known as Guinness & Company, wl [barcode, M000301924]
possible competition.

In Ireland, a lawyer discovered the unclaimed inheritance and found Billy in the United States to give him the money, minus his fee for the hours spent doing paperwork and finding the rightful heir. Billy was still left with a healthy portion, and he used it to build the finest home bar in the county. With the remainder, he kept the bar stocked for his friends. Not surprisingly, the number of friends Billy had doubled every year for quite some time.

To cut down on his costs, Billy worked with the town council to start a regular event where people would start at his house for a few drinks, walk together to The Night's Quest for free food, and then head to Hank's Tavern to end the night listening to the best country and rock bands in the area. He hoped it would be a subtle way to get people to spend more time at the real bars where they would spend their own money—instead of Billy's—to get drunk. Eventually, he planned to phase his house out of the rotation altogether. The bar crawl caught on and was popular for decades, but Billy still ran out of money and had to sell his home to a husband and wife who turned it into The Mancheville Pub.

George Miranda wasn't particularly interested in theories about why the local drink sippers and beer sluggers went to the three places in the same order every night. The mayor died of liver failure even though he quit the sauce. The only ghosts that George ever saw wore sheets and asked for candy on Halloween. Billy McDevitt spent the money from selling his home bar to return to his roots in Ireland. Nobody ever heard from him again. Even Patrick, his brother, who still lived in Mancheville, never spoke with him again. Patrick was the youngest child in the family and was only eight when Billy made his trip to Ireland. If Billy had returned to family members in Ireland, Patrick didn't know them.

George was a fairly regular participant in the nightly bar trifecta, despite not caring much about why folks did it the way they did. He did it because it was comfortable. Like most seventy-year-olds, George knows what is comfortable to him and is content to stick to those activities. He enjoys having a few drinks but rarely gets noticeably drunk.

He typically felt like his place was squarely in the center of all the people he ever knew. Whether it was politics, religion, types of beer, or musical genres, he always seemed to end up in the middle of varying opinions. His propensity towards seeing both sides of an issue or argument gave him the reputation of being fair, wise, and judicious. Unfortunately, seeing both sides of things also made him something of a moderator for conflicts between friends and acquaintances.

There seemed to be an effusive pressure that George couldn't quite put his finger on. An odd blend of simmering sensitivity and sectarian aggression had overtaken the town. It was a bizarre situation where opinions were so strong and emotions so intense that many folks had become exhausted and withdrawn from civility. Between those with differing views, common ground was harder and harder to find. Rationality was wilting, and the decay was producing nothing more than poison gas–a pressure that was simultaneously powerful and fruitless. More than anywhere else, it was seeping from the windows of the bars in Mancheville.

CHAPTER TWO

The sneakers have this peculiar and glorious bulk to them that looks both light and heavy at the same time. From every angle, there are curves like an old Cadillac with none of the hardness. The bumpers are foamy and riddled with indulgent rolls and bevels that serve no purpose. It's hard to distinguish if they're made of fake leather or cheap real leather smoothed down to a weird texture. They have dozens of separate sections stitched together. They are a blinding, bleachy white that's only interrupted by a logo or a brand wordmark embroidered in a boring font with all capital letters.

The only selling point that matters to George is that they're damned comfortable. He occasionally made an effort to be stylish and avoid looking obviously old, just to retain the last string connecting him to youth. He might wear a pair of jeans that fit a little slimmer than he'd prefer. Once in a while, he even bought patterned shirts like the ones college kids wore at the mall. He's okay with going a little bolder than his regular solid shirts to improve his fashion. But George drew the line firmly at the ankles. Foot comfort is simply too important to sacrifice in the name of vanity.

George liked to get showered, fully dressed and put on his sneakers before sitting in his deer-colored Nubuck leather office chair. His minimalistic wooden desk was just off his kitchen in the dining room. He'd sold the larger kitchen table that he owned with Anna and bought a tiny one from Ikea to accommodate for the desk in the corner and a rubbery plastic chair mat that allowed him to roll around. It was less of a dining room and more of an open-air office of sorts.

Many people in a long-term relationship, even those in healthy and successful partnerships, tend to have quick daydreams about what they would be doing if they were suddenly allowed to use all of their time exactly how they want. Those people's partners might be surprised to learn that often the only desire their mate has is to sit in silence without being asked why it's so quiet. Or just eat hot dogs between pieces of bread without being pressured into running to the store for hot dog rolls. Maybe sleep sideways on a bed for no damn reason at all. Dreams of guilt-free sex, lavish cars, and luxurious mansions? That's all fine, but the real dream, for some, is to be allowed a few glorious moments of complete autonomy each day.

George missed so much about Anna. They had a mostly wonderful marriage that produced children and grandchildren. They traveled quite a bit, had jobs where they both felt valued, worked together to get to a place of decent financial shape so they could retire, and loved each other faithfully until she passed away a few years into a struggle with ovarian cancer. In addition to their successes together, he missed the myriad of pleasant personality characteristics Anna possessed.

But George does not miss her asking him every morning why he insists on getting completely dressed and putting on sneakers before he does anything else. Maybe it is a little quirky on days when he knows he isn't leaving the house. He could just keep his pajamas on or at least wear slippers around the house. But it doesn't affect anybody else, and it helps him wake up. Anna had badgered him about it anyway. In a way, he almost recalled her pestering fondly. Almost.

George clicked his mouse quickly a few times, and the tower on the floor beside his desk whirred for a few moments before settling into a soothing idle. The computer monitor came alive and showed a picturesque shot of a clear mountain lake surrounded by rocks and trees with summer green leaves. A small block in the middle of the screen requested his log-in password. He typed 'aMARILLIS22'— Anna's favorite flower and lucky number—into the box and firmly hit the ENTER key with his pinky. His fingers always ended up confused and intertwined in weird ways as he used a hunt-and-peck method of typing. Even with typewriters, he'd never learned to type properly, so he relied on the less-efficient method of poking at the keyboard with no particular strategy for what finger typed what letter. It wasn't great, but he'd gotten pretty fast over the years, quick enough that he didn't feel the need to learn about home keys.

Like most mornings, he checked his email, looked at a few stocks that he had a marginal amount of money invested in, and checked the box score of the previous night's Phillies game. Even if he'd watched the game the night before, he often fell asleep around the eighth inning. Or he'd miss the end while he was driving home from Hank's. He'd watched the entire game last night at Hank's, a great game for the Phils that ended up being an 11-1 win. He checked the box score online anyway because he liked looking at the numbers when they were successful.

A few years ago, George's only grandson, Ethan, had taught him many of the basics of navigating the internet, like getting an email address, using social media, how to (hopefully) avoid viruses, and other stuff. With Ethan's help and by toying around by himself, George had become pretty savvy at using the web. His abilities were particularly impressive for a seventy-year-old who was already an adult when computers were the size of entire buildings. He'd always been pretty open to new technology, and he was quietly proud that he could hold his own with many from the younger generations when it came to the online world.

George grabbed the plate beside his monitor that held two fried eggs and two pieces of wheat toast before doing anything else. He ate all of the food quickly but chewed each bite thoroughly. He hadn't been paying attention and put much more pepper on his eggs than usual. For a second, the excess pepper made his nose wrinkle up, but he didn't sneeze, which was a disappointment. He loved a good sneeze, and, frankly, it seemed like a decent way to start a day. When finished with the last bite of egg, he dropped his fork on the plate with an obnoxious clank and leaned back in his chair while wiping his mouth.

Another thing that Ethan had taught George was how to start a blog. He had never been much of a writer and had never kept a journal, but he'd read something about how it was good for older people to do daily writing to keep their brains sharp. Or at least slow the dulling, anyway. He'd tried a few weeks of writing by hand in a journal, but he felt a bit silly writing to only himself. Once he had learned a little from Ethan about being online, he asked about blogging. He liked the idea that he could write some of his thoughts and feel like it was out in a public space. He wasn't writing anything deeply personal, and even if he did, he didn't have a whole lot to hide anyway.

George was very aware that almost nobody read his blog. Ethan had inserted some code into his blog page that allowed him to track when people viewed his webpage. Known as analytics—as Ethan had made sure to teach him—this tool even gave him advanced information like how long viewers looked at his page and even how they got there. The internet amazed George, in general, but analytics completely fascinated him. Despite having only a few dozen views a month—half of them being family members or friends—George was delighted by looking at the graphs and percentages that showed their behavior in great detail. Besides being fascinated, he had to admit that it felt kind of powerful to see what people were doing without them knowing.

His process of crafting a blog post started with jotting down some notes on a legal pad. After that, he'd open a new Microsoft Word document, but it would stay blank for at least ten minutes after being opened. A new browser tab would be devoted to YouTube, where he selected a classical music playlist—Vivaldi or Bach. He'd place full ear-covering headphones on his head. After a few moments of pure listening with eyes closed, a couple more scribbles on the legal pad, a sip of coffee, then a longer sip of coffee, he'd finally type the first sentence. While working on a blog post, he tried to concentrate only on writing for two full hours. Whatever he had at the end of two hours is what he would copy and paste into his blog for the day. He'd go slightly over to clean it up and end it in a way that made sense, but he found that working for about two hours was the best way to write something clear without rambling on too much.

Similar to an "A" in Morse code, he took a dot and a dash of coffee and settled his fingers above the keyboard, and started tapping in his chaotic, unsystematic manner.

CHAPTER THREE

"Damn libtards," mumbled Don Keslowski while awkwardly twisting his hips and coming back through with his bulbous driver. It struck his golf ball with an ugly clanking sound. He grunted in a mixture of pain and disappointment as his golf ball flew into the pine trees to the left of the fairway. It pinballed between a few tree bases before finally coming to rest near a patch of poison ivy.

George let out a short laugh because it almost seemed like Don was blaming liberals for his poor drive. He wasn't. The exclamation was just a continuation of a conversation he'd been having with his cart passenger, Samuel Squire. The topic, which came up at least once each time they went golfing, was about how the local young progressives were destroying America. Specifically, the ones they often saw at the bars around town.

Patrick spoke up from the other golf cart after a long swallow of beer, "I think you'll be able to find your ball, Don, but you might want to stop for calamine lotion on the way home."

Don feigned anger and threw his broken tee at Patrick's bare shin below the hem of his shorts. It connected with a light smacking sound that made both of them laugh. He refocused back on Samuel and returned to their conversation.

"I just don't understand why the only thing they want to do is tear apart everything we care about," Don said while shaking his head in disgust. Samuel made some kind of motion with his head that was somehow both a nod of agreement and a disgusted side-to-side head shaking.

George tried his best to let all thoughts escape his mind while lining up to hit his tee shot. He had a smooth, abbreviated swing that only went about three-quarters of the way around his body and came through squarely most of the time. If he didn't rush it trying to swing hard, he usually hit a right to left draw that caught the fairway's edge or ended up a few yards into the left rough. He could immediately tell it was a decent swing, and he was satisfied to see his ball land in the fairway and just trickle into the taller grass. Short of the kidney-shaped fairway bunker and resting about 140 yards from the center of the green, eight-iron distance for George.

He walked off the tee box and stuck his driver back into his golf bag, wiggling it until it went the whole way down to the bottom. He slid into the golf cart's passenger seat beside Patrick and touched his knuckles to the knuckles on Patrick's extended right hand.

"Nice ball, bud."

"Thank you, sir," George responded pleasantly while pulling his can of beer from the cup holder to take a healthy gulp. Undoing the Velcro on his golf glove, he gently tugged on each leather finger, finally pulling it off by the index finger. He tossed it casually into the little cutout where he kept his balls and tees. Patrick stomped the gas pedal, sending the golf cart flying forward, and George leaned back to enjoy the whoosh of air on his cheeks and temples.

At the next tee, they had to wait for a moment for the group ahead of them. This annoyed Don, even though he was easily the slowest player in their group. As he often did, Samuel followed Don's lead and made it clear he was annoyed at the delay by muttering curses while staring at the players ahead of them. George cleaned the grooves on his sand wedge with a tee while Patrick smoked a cigarette and took a few quick nips from his flask. Don finally turned his attention away from the foursome ahead and saw Patrick with both hands full. He pulled his golf ball from his pocket and tossed it underhand towards Patrick's chest, and yelled, "Catch!"

Patrick only saw the ball at the last minute and was startled by the ball flying at him. He dropped his cigarette just in time to bat the ball away before it hit him. He stooped down to pick it up and jokingly exclaimed, "Damn it, Don, ya made me get pesticides all over my freakin' cigarette!" He picked up Don's ball and acted like he was going to throw it in the woods. "It's just gonna end up there, anyway," Patrick said with a laugh. He tossed it back to Don, who was clear to hit his tee shot.

Don proceeded to shank another shot left, this time into a field of waist-high grass that swallowed up golf balls as if it needed them for sustenance. Their foursome didn't have to wait anymore for the rest of their round because Don played some of the worst golf of his life from that point forward.

George ended up shooting an eighty-four, a very solid score for him. Their foursome—George, Don, Samuel, and Patrick—played once or twice almost every week at Running Brook Golf Course on the outskirts of Mancheville. George usually shot about a ninety on a typical day, so he was satisfied with his round. Samuel and Patrick had left to go home, so it was only George and Don at the club-house's small oval bar. They were the only customers at the bar. George wanted to grab a sandwich, and Don was still drinking beers even though he'd managed to get drunk during their round of golf.

Don was back on the younger crowd that they often spent time with at the local bars. He was trying his best to get George to engage and join him in complaining. "I'm not even political like those liber-als at Hank's. I have my own beliefs, and I care about my country. Nobody tells me what to believe."

George knew this wasn't true and that Don spent at least three hours a day watching the conservatively biased news network that he loved. Not only that, but his behavior on social media also betrayed him. Maybe deep down, he wasn't political, but he sure participated in a lot of partisan nonsense and was significantly altered by it. But George didn't feel like starting an argument. When George only shrugged and didn't join in bashing the young folks, Don gave up and returned to sipping his beer. George glanced up at the television to watch the baseball highlights. It was an off day for the Phillies.

After several minutes of silence, Don turned to George again. In a calmer voice than what he used when ranting about politics or twenty-one-year-olds, he said, "My daughter had this picture of her two boys on the front step from Halloween last year. She just found it when she was cleaning behind the refrigerator. It just killed me. They both dressed up as Spiderman. Originally, the oldest wanted to be a pirate, but he changed his mind at the last minute. My daughter had to go out and find the best Spiderman costume she could find with only one day until Halloween and not much money."

Don sipped the last of the beer in front of him and put a coaster on top of it to signal that he didn't want a refill. George took a large bite of his sandwich and chewed heartily.

Don continued, "The only one she found was baggy and loose and just didn't look quite right. The mask was way too big for his face, and he was looking through the nose holes instead of the eye-holes, and his little nose was poking out of the slit where his mouth was supposed to go. It looked ridiculous, but in a cute way, of course. He and his brother stood so proudly in their costumes. The youngest looked at least close to Spiderman because they had purchased his costume weeks before Halloween when they had time to try on different styles and sizes to find the perfect one. It had these fake muscles that looked pretty cool. Despite the big difference in costume quality, they both seemed equally happy.

"The oldest one wasn't self-conscious about his costume, and I think he felt like he looked awesome. He may have looked at his brother in his better costume and assumed he looked exactly like him. Maybe he didn't really think about it much at all and just thought he was freakin' Spiderman.

"I instantly had this sad feeling and cried a little because I couldn't stop thinking about when the first time would be they'd feel real disappointment. I don't mean not getting pizza for lunch or having to stop playing video games for the night, or stuff like that. I mean some heavy real-life shit. At some point, they're going to have to feel that sadness and despair. And it rips me up, George. It hurts that I just don't know how to stop that. That stupid picture got me going like that. I'm getting old or something."

George instantly felt a wave of relief that Don had switched to a less inflammatory conversation. It felt much more like the Don he had known for decades before he'd crafted some kind of image of himself as a defender of truth in a made-up battle against millennials. George still appreciated his friend, and most of the time, their interaction had nothing to do with any of that shit.

"Well, I've had similar feelings. It's happened to me with my grandkid, the same way you're experiencing it. Not that there wasn't plenty of tough stuff to get through raising a kid, but I think you're just so involved and consumed with your own kid that you don't get as philosophical about it. With grandkids, you have more time to think about stuff. It's nice to be a little detached because you can spoil them and treat them in ways you couldn't with your own. But it also feels a bit helpless because you see all of the same dangers and sadness and pain, but you're not the one that gets to protect them.

"I guess you just have to realize that all of that hard stuff won't hit in one crippling impact. It'll happen in small doses so they can learn to deal with it the same way all of us do. They'll be damaged, but then they'll get to realize what it means to heal."

Don got up and patted George on the shoulder. He looked George in the eye and said sluggishly but sincerely, "Thanks, buddy.

You're a damn wise man, sometimes." He walked towards the bathroom and stumbled on the rug in front of the door with the male stick figure on it. He didn't fall, but he did let out a loud guffaw at his inebriated lack of grace. Don was drunk, but he'd taken in what George had said, and George knew it.

CHAPTER FOUR

It's a pretty great time of the day to tend bar. When people are getting off work or done with their errands, they stop at the bar to let off some steam and breathe a little bit. It's always calm, and rarely is anybody drunk or out of control yet. There are fewer spills and less impatience. Happy hour isn't always the most lucrative time for a bartender, but it is pleasant. The Mancheville Pub was filling up, but it was still relatively tranquil for the staff.

Behind the bar, the pub's newest bartender was cutting limes and humming to the soft rock song that emanated from the speakers hung in the corners of the bar. The pub had gone through eight-track players, stereos, boom boxes, satellite radios and was now just using the smartphone of whoever was bartending. The speakers had serviced all of the different devices for nearly forty years without a single problem. If there was ever a break in the music, it was because somebody had accidentally yanked a wire or the device itself was malfunctioning. The owner, Nick, religiously dusted the speakers every Thursday night, just as he had when he was a child, and his parents owned the bar. As a youngster, he didn't mind the task of getting on a ladder and tediously cleaning the speakers because he loved getting a close-up look at the expensive speakers his father had convinced his mother were a good investment. Now, the dusting was just something he did without really thinking about it. His father was right, and they still sounded great.

Eventually, customers would mildly complain about the playlist the bartender used to relax before it got too busy. She'd switch it to classic rock or country depending on who was at the bar. It didn't bother her since she liked just about anything except for jazz and intense techno. Nobody had said anything, but she switched over to a heavier rock playlist so she wouldn't have to fumble around with her phone while trying to serve drinks. Sometimes she'd get dirty looks from older customers who thought she was answering a text or scrolling social media when she was just trying to appease another customer by changing the music. Little headaches like that came with the territory, though.

The Mancheville Pub hadn't changed much since Billy had sold it to Nick's parents. They'd kind of remodeled in the eighties but had used extra materials that Billy had safely stored in a shed, where it was protected from weather and wear. The ugly wood paneling was removed from the pub walls, only to be replaced by a less-worn version of the same paneling. It was a slightly different shade from not having absorbed cigarette smoke for a few decades, but it wasn't much different. They added a drop ceiling but painted the tiles the same brown shade as the sheetrock. The high-tops, dining tables, chairs, and stools had all been carefully refinished by Nick's father. Still, they didn't look much different because he'd found surplus wood stain in a metal cabinet in the shed—leftovers from the first refinishing of the furniture years before.

Older folks loved that the place they went to decades before felt almost the same. Younger customers laughed at the outdated design, but most also had affection for the charm of a place that didn't try to be anything more than it was.

Don's hair was still wet and freshly combed. He sat waiting patiently for a drink, poking at the screen of his phone that lay flat on the bar.

"How can I help you, Mr. Don?" asked the bartender with a genuine smile. Don was a regular customer and was always very sweet to her. She'd heard that he tended to get a little less sweet as the night went on, and his courtesies turned into awkward behavior with female bartenders. Though, all she knew of him was the respectful guy who frequently started his nights at The Mancheville Pub. She had no complaints, although she'd only been there for about six months.

"Just a beer will do, thanks!"

"No bourbon tonight?" He typically got his evening rolling with a pint of beer and a shot of Jim Beam—or sometimes new bourbon they were testing out.

"Got pretty tanked at the golf course yesterday. Gonna take it a little easier tonight. Sticking with only beer helps."

"Understood, that's very disciplined of you!" She said with a smile. They both laughed at the idea that being disciplined meant drinking beer all night.

"You know how I like to watch my drinking!"

"I think you've told me. Hold on, don't tell me. You like to watch your drinking ... you like to watch the glass empty and then watch it get refilled again!"

"They better keep you around; you're a quick learner."

They both laughed again while she turned to grab a pint glass. She stuck it under the tap of the light beer that Don preferred. She gently pulled the tap handle and let the foam fill the entire glass and finally overflow. After a few times through the process, it finally filled with pale golden liquid and only had a frothy head on the last half inch. She carefully moved the full glass over to the coaster that he'd already placed in front of himself.

"Thank you very much. I'll just pay in cash as I go. I'm not sure how long I'll be sticking around." Don slid a twenty-dollar bill to her. She made quick change, and he immediately handed her back two dollars.

"And thank you. Enjoy! I'll be helping out serving the trivia people. Don't hesitate to get my attention if you need anything."

Trivia was a new thing they'd started at the pub a few years ago— a way to get more customers in on weekday nights. Trivia night annoyed Don. The bar was for drinking, in his opinion, not about playing silly games for a twenty-five-dollar gift certificate that five people had to split. People seemed to enjoy it, but it all felt very odd to him. It partially annoyed him because it brought out a lot more people that he found pretentious. College students, yes, and older people who were supposedly educated, who cared more about theories from books than real-world common sense. Nobody was directly rude to him. They didn't interact with him at all, for the most part. They did have loud conversations where they seemed to dissect and pick apart the stupidest things and overcomplicate them. Don tried his best to ignore their babbling, but he couldn't help it sometimes. He knew his attitude was a little unfair, but he couldn't help feeling intruded upon by them.

Don's annoyance be damned; trivia night was happening.

"Yo, Mo!"

The shouted greeting came from one of the tables that pissed off Don. They had a group of five that came to trivia almost every week. The group consisted of two students from the community college close to Mancheville, a young couple in their twenties, and a professor from the college.

The source of the shout was one of the male students named Alonso Kent. His greeting was to his friend, Muhammad Darwish, who had just walked in the door with his girlfriend, Erin Agnew. They both sheepishly waved, slightly embarrassed at Alonso yelling over the din of the room.

"We have a pitcher and glasses for you and Erin, so you don't need to get anything at the bar!"

Muhammed—more commonly known as Mo to his friends—and Erin made their way to the table where Alonso was sitting with Professor Alfredson and a quiet female student named Kate. They scooched the chairs around until everybody had enough space to be comfortable. Alonso poured out two heady beers and passed them to Mo and Erin. Once they had their beers, Alonso clanked glasses with each of them.

The guy running the trivia game had his sound system set up and all the levels checked. He put his microphone up to his mouth, took a deep breath, and announced in his best radio voice, "Okay, folks! Welcome to The Mancheville Pub. Thanks for coming out to trivia night on this wonderful Wednesday evening! If you haven't played before, please pay close attention to the rules. Your team can be as large as you want, as long as everybody sits at one table. You can still play if you're at the bar, but we have to cap those teams at four people, so it doesn't get crazy up there. Please do not use any electronic devices to look up answers or phone a friend. Please refrain from shouting out any answers. That includes those of you who aren't playing. One person should be in charge of writing all of your answers on your sheet. Make sure to choose a name and put it at the top of your paper for each round. When I come through after each round, please promptly finish what you're writing and hand it over so we can keep it moving at a reasonable pace. We're playing for a twenty-five-dollar gift certificate to the pub for first-place, a box of king-size Snickers for second-place, and Bud Light keychains for everybody on the third-place team! Tonight's round categories will be sports, U.S. presidents, and music. If nobody has questions, let's get started!"

There was a mild buzz throughout all of the tables until the trivia guy quieted everybody down by shushing them and patting the air in front of himself to signal that they should lower their volume. When they finally did, he began with an easy question for anybody that even remotely followed sports.

"This Yankees player came under fire when he tested for steroids in the early 2000s. While playing for the Yanks, he wore number 13 and was known by the nickname 'A-Rod.' What is this player's real first and last name?"

Nearly every team's scribe began writing within seconds of the finished question, including Alonso's team. They had a mini fist-pumping celebration, happy to have known the first answer. Alonso took a healthy gulp from his beer and grabbed a French fry from the basket they all shared. One of the safer menu items at the pub. They could fry things pretty well, but that was where the culinary skills ended. Only Alonso and the professor had taken swigs large enough to put a dent in their beers. Alonso topped both of their pint glasses off, leaving only half a centimeter of beer in the bottom of the pitcher. He let that drip into Mo's glass until no more came out. With a flourish, he waved the empty pitcher in the direction of the bartender—not necessarily rude, but also not the preferred method of simply waiting for the waitress or bartender to make their rounds. Even so, the bartender didn't give him any attitude about the way he beckoned her. She grabbed the empty pitcher and filled it at the tap, patiently waiting for some of the head to crawl over the side and disappear into the little trough underneath the taps. She delivered the pitcher back to Alonso with a smile.

Back at the bar, Don sat with an empty glass, eating from a bag of pretzels he'd snagged from a clip on the wall. Regulars knew that it was okay to grab a bag of snacks and pay for it later.

The bartender returned and said to Don, "Wow, I didn't notice it before, but you got a hell of a lot of sun on the golf course yesterday! You're fire engine red, man!"

Don smiled, happy to be talking to the friendly bartender instead of just listening to the droning trivia guy. "That's what happens to old pasty men when they have too many beers and a few pulls from Patrick's flask. Ya forget to put on the sunblock ya packed in your golf bag and get burned up." He held out his arm and groused, "Of course, Pat, Sam, and George all forgot to put on sunblock, and they just got tanner," and added sarcastically, "I'm just lucky, I guess."

"Another beer?"

"Sure. I think that'll be my last one here."

"Okay. You're not gonna leave before trivia is over, are ya?" She smiled knowingly, aware that the trivia annoyed Don.

He rolled his eyes. "I just come for the alcohol. That's enough for me."

A half-hour later, Don was finished with his beer and stood up to stretch his back, preparing to move on to the next place. He grabbed a cocktail napkin from a plastic container on the bar that bore an outdated and almost totally faded Budweiser logo. He wiped his mouth while listening to the trivia guy ask the third to last question of the U.S. Presidents round.

"Which American president owned a home named 'Wheatland' on the outskirts of Lancaster city in Pennsylvania? He owned it until his death in 1868 when his niece inherited the building."

Don had to pass through some of the tables to exit the pub. The looks on the faces at the table to his left made it clear that nobody had a clue what the answer was. In contrast, Alonso was sitting at the table to Don's right with a smug smile on his face. Erin finished writing their answer and held out a thumbs-up to the table. Alonso, still grinning, waved to Don as he slowly passed. Don gave a weak wave back without smiling.

Don couldn't help himself. He stopped moving towards the door and sauntered over to the table of people he didn't know and whispered "Buchanan" into the ear of the guy with the answer sheet in front of him. The guy looked around, unsure what to do, but reluctantly wrote down what Don had told him, which happened to be the correct answer. Don walked out without looking back at Alonso and his team.

The Night's Quest hadn't started with a focus on food, but it had evolved over the years as ownership changed. It was originally just a barroom with a long cherry bar. Over the years, as it had grown into a dining establishment as much as a drinking establishment, they'd remodeled several times to accommodate more tables. And larger tables. A brief period with a petite salad bar that everyone hated. A new fireplace. A small stage for solo musical acts (the dinner crowd didn't care for full bands). The most recent remodel came with spacious modern bathrooms.

Due to all of the remodels and a concern for maintaining a regular flow of food customers, The Night's Quest was easily the cleanest and most updated food and drink establishment in Mancheville. The speakers were the cleanest thing at The Mancheville Pub, and the closest thing to a full cleaning that Hank's had in thirty years was when the basement flooded. They'd removed everything from the place and put it in the trailer of an eighteen-wheeler while they scrubbed, rinsed, and dried everything with blowers. Even then, it wasn't what you'd call a thorough sanitizing job. So, The Night's Quest is the most trustworthy place to have a meal.

Steak night at The Night's Quest was no joke. It was always the busiest night during the week. They offered six cuts of steak, which was three more than what was on the standard menu. Of those cuts, one was a six-ounce filet mignon that was considered the best in the county. The quality was so good that customers regularly suggested to their server that it should become a regular menu item. Only one waitress on staff had been around long enough to remember when they'd tried to make it a regular menu item for about half a year. Once it wasn't on special, they sold almost none of it and had to make a weekly donation to the local food bank because of all the extra meat. Now, when customers suggested adding filet mignon to the menu, waiters and waitresses just agreed and nodded, told them they'd talk to the manager, or just put an 'I don't know' look on their face.

Patrick and his wife were nearly done with their meal when Don walked in and found them at a table in the dining area corner. When he came to their table, he looked at their plates, sizing up the remains, and pointed first at Patrick's plate. "Ribeye with a baked potato and broccoli." He swung his finger over to Charlene's plate and proclaimed, "Filet mignon with mashed potatoes and a side of applesauce."

Patrick looked up at him with amused eyes and answered, "Close. You got mine right, but not Char's. They were out of applesauce, so she got some cucumber thing instead."

"Cucumber salad, dear," Charlene said.

"Yeah, that. She rinsed two of the slices off in her water glass and put them in a Ziploc bag in her purse. She's gonna wear 'em on her eyes and lay in the bathtub tonight. Saves us money since she doesn't have to go to the spa."

Charlene couldn't help but giggle but followed it with, "Oh, shut it. Quit telling lies and drink your whiskey, Patrick."

Don laughed and pulled out one of the two extra seats at their table to sit down. Their waiter had seen Don join Patrick and Charlene and came over from a different table. "Evening, Don. Would you like a drink? Do you need a menu?"

"No, thanks, Andy. I'll grab something at the bar in a little when I move there. Just visiting this handsome couple."

"Sounds good." Andy turned to the other two and asked, "Do you two need anything else while I'm here?"

Charlene answered, "I think we're all set. We'll take our check so we can leave a tip for you. If we move to the bar, we'll start a new tab."

"Excellent, I'll be right back with that."

Andy made his way towards the kitchen, taking diminutive steps on his tippy toes that made it look like he was wearing an invisible pair of pumps. He held his tray in one hand while popping the kitchen door with the heel of his hand. His tray hand strayed behind him and dodged the closing door with a dramatic flourish at the last second.

Still looking at the closed kitchen doors, Don remarked, "Andy is a good server, but he seems really queer. Do ya think he's a homo or somethin'?"

Patrick, not seeming too interested in the question, replied, "Probably somethin'. A lot is going on with the younger crowd these days. Things I never even heard of before. I don't know."

Charlene jumped in like she'd been waiting weeks to share the information she had. "He has a boyfriend. I'm on the town parade committee with his grandmother. She doesn't seem overly concerned about the whole thing. I guess he's happy, and that's all she cares about. I suppose that is how I would be."

"So just a regular gay?" questioned Don

Neither Patrick nor Charlene answered as both were finishing sips of their respective drinks. Don wished he'd ordered a drink on their dinner tab and just paid them back later at the bar.

Patrick finally answered, "Regular gay, I guess. Whatever that means. He's a fella who loves a fella. I don't really think about it, I guess. It's his business."

"I just don't get it. How do two guys kiss and touch each other? And more that I won't even mention here!"

Patrick dabbed his mouth with his napkin and gave Don a serious look. He readjusted himself in his chair, turning towards Don, and said, "Don, if this is your strange way of asking me to drop Charlene and disappear to a tropical island somewhere, the answer is no. Just to keep my options open, though, how much money do you have in the bank, and how much of that are you willing to spend on my drinking habit without complaining as much as Charlene?"

Don laughed uncomfortably and punched Patrick on the arm. "Shut up, ya jackass!"

Patrick guffawed, and Charlene rolled her eyes, quipping, "You two deserve each other!"

Andy bounced up to their table and delicately laid the check holder in the middle of the table. "I'll take that when you're ready!"

"You don't have to leave; here ya go." Patrick already had a credit card in his hand and immediately stuck it in the holder.

Andy grabbed it and said, "I'll take care of that right away."

Less than a minute later, he returned. Patrick carefully wrote in a tip and scribbled his signature. The three of them stood up and started towards the bar. On the way, Andy thanked them, and both Patrick and Charlene responded in kind.

The three of them moved to the bar and settled in three of the five empty stools. It wasn't a large bar; there were only a dozen places to sit in total. The original cherry bar that stretched nearly the whole room had been modified into a smaller square bar. It was a compact area that one bartender could handle most of the time.

Don, did you hear about Jim Gentzler?"

"I didn't; what happened?"

"He had a heart attack on Monday. Right in his driveway. Which was a blessing because he didn't make it into his truck and drive anywhere." Charlene shook her head sadly. "They think he'll be okay, though. He's still in the hospital now to rest and get some tests, but he'll be home again soon. No work for a while."

Patrick was only half paying attention, as he already knew about Jim and was in the process of getting the bartender's attention.

Don was listening, as Jim had been an old high school friend. He only saw him occasionally these days, but they were friendly. He responded, "I can't believe how freakin' old we are, Charlene." He grabbed the beer that Patrick slid in his direction and sipped just enough so it wasn't filled to the very top. "You have heart attacks when you're still working manual labor at seventy-three. He's nuts, but I guess he doesn't have much of a choice. It's a damn shame that freakin' bums out there collect welfare, and an old man who worked all his life isn't even taken care of. What the hell's wrong with the world?"

Patrick handed Charlene her highball glass and settled onto his stool with his rocks glass of whiskey. He remarked, "We saw his sister at the pub earlier. Were you there? We must have just missed you."

Don snorted. "I was there after you. I wasn't there too long. I don't care to listen to the damn trivia game they play."

Patrick laughed. "I don't know; I think it's all kind of funny. I'd play if somebody got a group together. It would have to be all history or old shit for me. I can remember stuff from years ago, but I can barely remember what I had for breakfast this morning. I feel like I'm playing trivia when Charlene asks me what day of the week it is."

"He's a little dramatic, but we both have our brain fart moments. I looked for my lost cell phone for an hour and a half yesterday before realizing it was in my back pocket." She motioned with one hand as if to say, 'oh well,' and drank her club soda and vodka with her other hand.

Don silently scrolled on his phone while Patrick and Charlene talked about a variety of topics, not seeming to care if Don was listening or not. They went back to Jim's heart attack and the various bad habits that lead to it. First, they discussed his diet and concluded that having cheeseburgers and fried mozzarella sticks as staples of your diet was probably not a good idea. Patrick mentioned that although Jim had stopped smoking for three years or so, he went back into his daily two-pack routine when he'd lost his job at the paper mill and gotten bored during the day while looking for a new job. Patrick also openly wondered how much damage he and Jim had done to themselves with the speed that they used to take to play football games. Although discussing possible heart damage, Patrick seemed to fondly remember taking the amphetamine pills—or pink hearts as they called them—when they were only teenagers.

Charlene, tired of talking about Jim and his heart attack, gave the details of a bingo event that their church held to benefit a mission trip that the youth group was taking the next summer. The bingo would be to win designer purses donated by a nearby outlet store.

Neither guy paid much attention other than an occasional head nod and a 'yeah' confirmation to give the appearance that they were listening. Don watched the television behind the bar and grimaced at the liberal news show that was playing. There was no sound, but it had closed captioning. In between poor text translations of the verbal dialogue that were so bad they just seemed like gobbledygook, a coherent sentence would flash, slamming the conservative president, pointing out some supposed act of racism, or promoting gun control that would spike Don's blood pressure briefly.

Don sipped his beer and moved his gaze from the television to the front door when he heard the bell attached to it jingle to signal that somebody was entering.

The person entering was Alonso, with Mo and Erin in tow. Either trivia was over, or they'd left early. They'd most likely walked from the pub, as they were all visibly sweating. Even Erin, who was thin, fair-skinned, and usually quite delicate, had beads of perspiration clinging to her temples and cheeks. They made their way to the bar, where Mo grabbed a short stack of cocktail napkins and passed them out to Alonso and Erin while keeping a few. All three blotted their faces to absorb the coating of sweat that had developed. Erin was more careful than the two guys and gently dabbed around her eye makeup. Alonso collected their now wet and ripped napkins and mushed them into one tight ball. He leaned over the bar and searched for the large square trash can he knew was somewhere near the dishwasher. When he located it, he firmly pitched the balled mess into it.

The bartender greeted the trio with a warm smile and said, "Hey guys! Are you here for steak night? Do you need menus, or are you just having drinks tonight?

Alonso didn't hide his annoyance with the bartender's questions. After a dramatic eye roll, he complained, "C'mon, you ask me that every time I'm in on steak night. Every time you ask me if I'm here to eat steak, I tell you that I'm a vegetarian. I haven't had a single piece of meat in four years, much less a big disgusting steak with a bunch of fat and dripping grease. Yuck."

As was usually the case, Mo took the much more straightforward approach and said no thanks to menus and that they'd just be having drinks. Erin smiled sheepishly at the bartender, subtly apologizing for Alonso's obnoxious response.

The bartender wasn't thrown off and answered back, "Oh, of course. I can't believe I always forget. What are you guys drinking tonight?"

Alonso still seemed annoyed, and seeing Don seated on a stool at the bar didn't help his mood. He turned to Mo and Erin and asked, "I don't feel like hanging out here. Let's just do a shot and bounce. I'll drink whatever you guys want if that's okay with you."

Mo and Erin both shrugged, and Erin answered, "That's cool. We can just head straight to Hank's after a shot. Let's do a lemon drop!"

Mo already had his credit card in hand and casually held it out to the bartender. "Three lemon drops, please. Also, a glass of water and the check for all three shots."

"Coming right up!"

The bartender handled the shaker of vodka like a maraca, trying his best to stay in time to the barely audible music playing. He had no future as a percussionist. From under the bar, he pulled up three shot glasses with one hand, flipping his hand awkwardly to turn them right side up. He poured the chilled vodka into each glass, careful to keep them all even. Once completed, he used tongs to pluck three lemon wedges from a rectangle container sectioned into four square areas. One held orange wedges, the next maraschino cherries, the third olives, and the last one lemon wedges. He placed the three lemon wedges on a small plate and let the container lid fall with a loud pop. He took a half scoop of sugar from a medium-sized plastic cylinder and dumped it on a neat pile on the plate. He slid the plate near the shots, smiled at the three watching him, and said excitedly, "Oh yeah!"

They thanked him, and all reached for their shots. They lifted the tiny glasses in the air before lightly tapping them on the bar surface and tossing them between their lips. Alonso let both Mo and Erin grab a lemon wedge and dab it in the plate's sugar. He followed after them, and they all stood looking ridiculous with lemon wedges in their mouth like wax teeth, doing their best not to laugh and spit out the lemon. They returned the mangled wedges to the plate, and each took a quick sip of water. Mo signed the check, and the three young friends left unceremoniously after doing their shots.

Don, Patrick, and Charlene were still working on their drinks at the other end of the bar.

Charlene tapped her mouth with a cocktail napkin and asked, "How is Paula? Have you talked to her much lately?"

Don let out a whoosh of air, a kind of signal that it wasn't a topic that he was particularly keen to talk about. "I talk to her as little as possible. Saw her a month ago at the grandkids' swim meet, but we only said hello to each other. I'm sure I'll be seeing her at Asher's soccer games in the fall. It's best if we avoid each other to keep it civil."

Don and Paula had divorced five years ago after a marriage consisting of one year of bliss, ten years of indifference, and another three of absolute misery and resentment.

Charlene paused for a moment but continued with what she had to say. "Is that really what's best for everybody—not saying anything to each other?"

Charlene periodically brought up their relationship in an attempt to at least get them to be friends again. It wasn't really for the couple's sake. Charlene was too nervous to talk to Paula after the divorce, even though they had once been good acquaintances, friends, even. Patrick was friends with Don before Paula, so it felt like they had to take a side as a couple. Which was silly, but it felt that way for some reason. Now, enough time had gone by that it would be way too uncomfortable to talk to her again suddenly. Her only hope was that Don would start communicating with Paula again, and she could use that as an icebreaker to talk to Paula again herself.

Patrick chewed on a piece of ice from his glass of whiskey, obviously a little annoyed by Charlene's line of questioning with Don. "Char, can you just drop it? I don't understand how you don't see that it's actually a mature thing for two divorced people to just give each other space without trying to bring up old shit at a kid's swim meet."

Charlene clammed up and silently sipped from her highball glass.

Don felt a little bad for Charlene, even though the questions were bothersome. Trying to lighten things up, he piped in, "Hey, it's okay. I don't know. Maybe someday things will be different." He couldn't help but add, "But for now, the bitch can watch from the other side of the pool."

Patrick, softening his tone, added, "Honey, I'm sorry, I didn't mean to be rude. I just know that it's not a pleasant subject for Donnyboy, here."

Charlene seemed to accept the apology and the tension left her face. She sucked on her straw, rattled her glass to settle everything, and took one last loud slurp to get the remaining club soda and vodka. She stood up and stretched, her subtly wrinkled but still toned arms thrusting out like she was testing her wingspan. "I'm going to head home. I'm tired. You boys enjoy Hank's and don't drink too much." She kissed Patrick on the cheek and lightly slapped his ass. She gave Don a gentle hug and patted him sweetly on the back.

Patrick smiled and said, "Good night, honey. Drive safe."

Don and Patrick ordered one more round of drinks after she left and drank them with almost no words to each other. They both surveyed the remainder of the dinner crowd, which was starting to thin out as it was now past ten o'clock. When a group of attractive young ladies appeared from behind a wall that had been blocking their view from the bar, Don and Patrick looked at each other with a knowing smile. The young women were on their way out, and when the door closed behind the last firm behind, Don and Patrick laughed like teenage boys.

"Maybe they'll be at Hank's later," Patrick said hopefully, adding, "Maybe you'll get yourself a date!"

Don looked at Patrick with a cynical smirk. "I think I might be a little out of their age range."

"Pfft, no such thing."

"That's what you say."

Patrick grinned slyly and said in a fake non-caring voice, "I guess you're still waiting around for that Hank's bartender to let you take her out. What's her name, Mary?" Patrick knew damn well what her name was, but he liked to mess with Don.

"I've never tried to date MEGAN," Don said, emphasizing her name. "I don't pretend she's my girlfriend or anything like that. So, what if I like to flirt with her when she's serving drinks? It's not a damn crime."

"I didn't say it was," Patrick said with his grin still plastered on his face. "We should get to Hank's, so we don't miss those young ladies if they stop there. Be quick with the rest of that beer."

"I'll drink my beer at whatever speed I please, thank you very much."

"I hear the beers taste better when Megan's pouring them."

Don pointed out his middle finger with the hand he was using to hold his glass while the rest clutched the glass. With exaggerated slowness, he lifted the glass towards his mouth. With his middle finger now directed straight upwards, he drank the beer as languidly as possible. He finished the rest of it without taking a breath and deliberately set down the glass. "Now, we go."

George entered Hank's to a hum of talk and activity. It was pretty bustling for a Wednesday night. He saw Patrick and Samuel at the bar's far corner, both waving lit cigarettes animatedly while they talked over Don sitting between them staring at his phone. To George's right, he saw Alonso, Mo, and Erin behind the row of taps that hovered over the bar like a little pipe organ. They were engaged in a friendly conversation with a middle-aged man and woman who seemed like they were probably married. From what George could hear, it sounded like they were having a lighthearted discussion about their favorite candy, each of them throwing out their personal top three. George pondered his own top three for a moment and came up with: Snickers, Twix, and Hershey's Almond. He'd have a quick answer if they happened to ask him.

In the back of the building, a lone musician was strumming a guitar and singing a song that George didn't recognize. He didn't recognize the guy either. He looked at his watch and saw it was ten minutes until eleven. Music usually ended at eleven 'clock unless the patrons demanded that whoever was playing be allowed to continue for more songs. George noted that this guy was okay but probably not good enough for anybody at the bar to cry out for an extended encore.

The only table with people at it held three pretty female faces that were not familiar to George. They each were sipping on a different dessert martini, and each sampled the others' drinks while maintaining a steady flow of unbroken conversation that was inaudible to George.

At the takeout case, an ancient fellow in a stained farm cap was studying the six-pack selection. George couldn't remember his name, but he knew what the old guy would eventually choose. If anybody offered, George would take even money for a hundred bucks that he'd carefully slide out a sixer of Old Milwaukee after a minute or two of browsing.

George glanced at the middle portion of the bar and saw an assortment of faces that seemed vaguely familiar but whom he'd never spoken to that he could remember.

Hank's had been a town staple for hundreds of years. George didn't know precisely when it had opened, but he knew it was one of the state's oldest drinking establishments. Probably even pretty high up there for the entire country. It had been through many proprietors. Different families had owned it over the years, but they kept the same name since it was a Mancheville institution. It was pretty remarkable that nobody had ever felt like they needed to revamp the old place and slap a new name on it.

Hank's was housed in a fairly large brick building with three stories. At one time, the top two floors were filled with livable rooms and apartments. Over time, the top floor ran into some disrepair and became uninhabitable. Now, nobody even went up there. The second floor was in decent shape, but the rooms were now just used for storage purposes. Save for one room, where the owner's brother had lived for at least twenty years. He was something of a casual property manager for the outside of the building. Depending on what was needed, he was also a janitor, cook, security, and even bartender in the most desperate situations. His real name was Arnold, but everybody called him Cookie. Other than Bob and their elderly mother in a nursing home, nobody knew why it was his nickname. In fifty years of knowing him, George had never bothered to ask.

George plopped down onto the stool next to Samuel and casually waved to the three guys.

Patrick stubbed out his cigarette in the half-full ashtray and said, "Well, George finally graces us with his presence tonight. Pleasure to see you, my friend!"

"Thank you, Patrick, same to you."

All three stuck out their hands, and George shook each one.

He settled back on the stool and rested his arms on the bar with his fingers intertwined. Megan finished serving a round of cocktails to the folks that George didn't know. She saw him while delivering the drinks and gave him a friendly nod.

Almost every other bartender in town was forgettable. Nice, but not exceptionally skilled enough that people thought of them as professional bartenders. Megan was the exception. Being a striking blonde with an hourglass figure and an ample chest helped, but she had the skills to back up her attractiveness. She was born in Mancheville but had lived in New York City for about ten years. She'd tended bar at a few different places in Manhattan. One of them was incredibly swanky, a couple were incredibly busy places that served thousands of customers each night, and the other was a Coyote Ugly rip-off where she had to dance on the bar once an hour. All of them were places where you had to be a skilled bartender with top-notch knowledge of cocktails and the ability to serve them quickly under pressure.

Megan had an off-and-on boyfriend for the last two years she was in New York City. He was a decent guy; no anger issues or cheating, or uncontrollable drinking. He was far from perfect, as he was lazy and not ready to be a father. Those aren't the world's worst sins, but they are a problem when you impregnate someone. That someone was Megan. Two months into her pregnancy, they broke up.

Megan decided that she'd like to raise her child back in Mancheville to provide him a calmer, more laidback childhood than New York City could offer. She opted to stay in the city for three more months. To his credit, her ex-boyfriend was okay continuing to live together to help her prepare for the move. He even scrounged up enough money each month to pay all of the rent so Megan could save more money for her future transition to Pennsylvania.

That was six years ago. Now Megan is the queen of Hank's and the favored bartender in Mancheville. Although not living high on the hog, it's enough to raise her only child without too much trouble.

From across the bar, Megan caught George's attention, pointed to the lager tap handle, and cocked her head in a questioning manner. Without a word, he gave her a smile and a thumbs up. He despised talking or yelling across the bar and avoided it at all costs. He waited patiently, staring at the tin ceiling with its intricate design repeated on each tile. He'd noticed that other bars now copied this style of ceiling with reproduction tiles. The square tiles in Hanks were old as hell; originals from when the style had first been popular. George was pretty sure they weren't original to the building but from at least as far back as the 1800s.

The walls at Hank's were half plaster, and half wood paneling painted so thick you can barely make out the grooves cut into it. The plaster had always been a consistent non-descript beige color, and the wood paneling was always some shade of brown that varied throughout the years. It seemed to mimic different kinds of beef-based soups. Sometimes it was beef vegetable with a hint of tomato paste, or it might be beef barley with an earthy tan influence; other times, it was like the deep beef stock broth of French onion soup.

Megan laid down a coaster and carefully sat his beer on it. She double-tapped the bar surface with the palm of her hand and gave him an affable wink. George raised his glass in her direction in a simple gesture of appreciation.

Samuel finished a sip of gin and tonic and released the slightest moan of pleased satisfaction. He looked over at George and asked, "What's new, buddy?"

"Oh, not a whole lot. Just a regular day, I suppose. I was watching the Phillies, and then I fell asleep for a few hours. Figured I'd come out for a few pints since I'm all rested."

"Did they win?" Samuel struck a match and lit a new cigarette.

"Honestly, I don't even remember the score when I fell asleep, and I never checked when I finally woke up."

Both laughed.

"Did you write a journal thing on the internet this week? What do they call it? A flog?"

"Blog. I did write one the other day."

"What was it about this time?"

"Ya know, a blog is public so people can read it. If you checked it out, you wouldn't have to ask me about it at the bar." George may have sounded a bit rude to a stranger, but he just liked to kid Samuel.

"Hey, anytime Debra pulls it up for me, I read it. I have to rely on the wife to do that shit for me. I just don't get it."

"I know, I know. I'm just yankin' your chain. You could learn it if you tried, though. You have enough brains to learn some simple stuff on the computer. You use Brainspot, don't ya?"

Samuel waved his hand dismissively. "My wife even pulls that up for me. She signs out of her page and logs me into mine. I know how to do the most basic stuff, and that's about it."

George continued, "Anyway, I wrote it before we went golfing. I just talked about how I'd like to practice chipping more because I always screw them up and lose dumb strokes during my rounds. I posted a couple of little drills from golf magazines that I did in the yard. It helped; I shot that 84 yesterday and I didn't hit a chip thin all day."

"That's great! I didn't even know what you shot, but I knew you were having a pretty decent round. Can't say the same for myself. Wasn't horrible, but it wasn't impressive."

"You were driving the ball well except for that one you sent out of bounds on seventeen."

"It's been said a billion times, but it's still true. Drive for show, putt for dough.

Don heard pieces of their conversation and said in a low voice, "Hey, speaking of golfing, do you recognize that guy over there?" He pointed towards the folks that Megan had just served a round of cocktails to, the people George didn't know. Don was pointing at the guy furthest away from them in the group, a thirtyish, well-built African American man in a stylish golf shirt.

"Can't say I do," George responded.

Don said quietly, "I think he used to be the pro over at West Hills Country Club before it closed down last year. Remember, my former brother-in-law worked on the maintenance crew there, and I was able to play there a few times. He introduced me to the pro, and I think that was the guy. Can't quite remember."

Samuel replied, "Why don't you just ask him?"

Don shrugged off the suggestion. "It's not that big of a deal. I was just wondering if maybe you guys knew him. I don't need to bother him about it."

George felt someone staring from across the bar and turned his head until he saw Alonso's eyes focused intently on Don. When Alonso finally broke his eye contact, he noticed George, and a more pleasant look came to his face. He tipped his head gently to greet George, who responded with a brief wave.

Don noticed the two exchanging greetings and spit out, "Ugh, that little prick. Kid annoys the hell out of me." He looked towards George in an attempt to disguise that he was talking about Alonso.

Don answered, "He's not so bad; I've talked to him plenty of times before in here. If you got to know him, you might not despise him so much. What's so awful about him?"

"For one, he's a liberal commie. You see the shit he posts online?" Don narrowed his eyes and added, "I can't stand these young entitled assholes."

Samuel jumped in to support Don. "He supports these politicians that just want to give away everything to the laziest people in society while they take from hard workers like us."

"George, you should have seen him cause a scene at the Night's Quest because the bartender asked if he was there for steak night. He made sure to announce to the entire bar that he's a vegetarian. So damn proud of himself for eating rabbit food. I'm not sure if I can talk to somebody that doesn't eat steak."

George couldn't help but sigh at their lamenting. "Maybe you guys are being a little melodramatic about the guy. He does differ with you about some political stuff. But he works and goes to his college classes, from what I've gathered. I think he wants to be a nurse. He's trying to do something with his life. Can't you ease up a bit?"

Samuel seemed willing to change the subject, but Don muttered, "Free college if he has his way."

George was relieved when Megan interrupted their discussion. "Sorry to disturb this meeting of the minds, but does anybody need anything?"

Don's mood immediately got brighter at the sight of Megan, and he held out his empty pint glass with a playful puppy dog look in his eyes. "More beer, please. I think I'm sober, and I don't like it."

"I think it's been a few years since you've had that problem, dear," she quipped. Nobody else answered, but she refilled everybody's drinks anyway except for George, who still had a mostly full glass.

The refill seemed to dissipate the little bit of tension that had built up. The singer went into a spirited rendition of Johnny Cash's "Folsom Prison Blues" that delighted everybody still at the bar. Several people, including Don, Patrick, and Samuel, started clapping as soon as the performer nailed the short guitar intro to the tune. George reconsidered his original estimation of him; maybe he would get those encore requests after all.

CHAPTER FIVE

Sometimes George had conversations with Anna beside her grave. Other times, like today, he just liked to be near it in silence. It was a classic Pennsylvania morning in August, which meant it was muggy as hell, and you sweated even though the sun wasn't even shining that brightly yet. There was no rhyme or reason to whether he talked not. He never even knew if he was going to speak to Anna until he arrived at her headstone.

The humidity seemed almost visible as George looked over the hundreds of stone markers arranged in imperfect lines over the ten-acre cemetery. Sometimes he'd walk the rows and stop at names that he was familiar with, which was a good many of them. Even if he hadn't known them personally, he probably knew one of their family members. At the very least, almost all of the names seemed to ring some kind of bell just because they were names that had been in Mancheville for multiple generations. And now, an increasing number of stones were people that had been the same age as George, and he'd known them very well. Growing old didn't make it any less strange to see the name of somebody that he remembered best as a fourth-grader, or somebody he'd played peewee baseball with, or a woman who had seemed impossibly beautiful and unattainable as a twenty-something but was now dead.

But George wasn't interested in walking around in the heat, so he wasn't finding any names that conjured up memories like that. He arrived and stood wordless in front of Anna's grave with an amaryllis flower drooping in his hand that was also not enjoying the oppressive heat. He laid the flower beside the granite block that bore her name, birth date, and date of death. He knelt and tried his best to position the flower to at least be in the shade of the stone as much as possible and hopefully last a little longer than if it was baking in the sun.

When he stood up, he noticed a chunky red button sitting on the top of the stone he hadn't seen before. It seemed very familiar to him, but he couldn't quite place it. Maybe it was an old friend who used to sew with Anna who put it there. Perhaps somebody had just lost their button near Anna's grave, and the cemetery caretaker had found it and placed it on her stone in case it was important to somebody. George stared at it for a few minutes, but he still wasn't sure where it might have come from despite it being oddly familiar.

George broke his concentration on the button and stared off into the woods that surrounded the cemetery. Two squirrels chased each other around the larger oak trees, and a few birds were scattered in the smaller trees. Within the trees, George could just make out the trail that had been carved out of the vegetation twenty or so years ago. Anna had been delighted when the town council allotted money to clear out a path for easy walking. Some folks, mostly bored teenagers, had walked the crude path for years before but had to battle briars and tree roots hidden under layers of leaves and dead branches. Once the path was cleared, the town supervisor did a pretty good job making sure somebody kept it safe and walkable. Anna and George had taken many strolls on the patch from one end of town to the other.

What had made their relationship work for almost forty years? There were countless fantastic memories, but just thinking about four decades of marriage was tiring. It almost didn't seem like it happened. Like it was a story, or a movie, that had lasted very long but now seemed like it had occurred in an instant. Sections had been incredibly difficult and seemed to drag so heavily at the time, but now just seemed like a chapter of only fuzzy remembrances.

They'd fought like bitter enemies sometimes early on when they were dating. Of course, every emotion has a passionate tinge to it early on in a relationship. That can manifest as anything from deep lust to screaming arguments. It was that way for a little. Eventually, George and Anna's relationship developed into a more understanding but also more calculated life together. Shouting lessened because of a better understanding of each other's personality and because mature people know that strategic barbs or passive aggression are much more effective ways to incense a life partner.

That's just the reality of spending time together. Mostly, it was a pleasant life that George experienced with Anna. They were both quirky but allowed each other those things that they couldn't possibly change. If they disagreed, they usually just accepted it and moved on. Plenty of times, disagreement just turned out to be them complementing each other.

Both of them had a small circle of friends that were very important to them. They both felt incomplete if they didn't see those people regularly and maintain a significant relationship with them. Both Anna and George trusted that time spent away from each other did not mean anything was wrong. In fact, it demonstrated much of what was right about their relationship—trust, understanding, lack of selfishness with time, and an appreciation for the qualities in each other that made others want to enjoy those qualities too.

Sometimes George cried in the cemetery. Sometimes he cursed into the air as long as nobody else was around. Today was mostly a stoic day, but he did smile briefly while reflecting on their companionship.

George decided to ignore the heat and walked the whole way to the other end of the cemetery to the tree line's edge. He paced along the edge for a few minutes to find the clearest route to the walking path. He finally came across a barely visible lane that deer probably used to get into the cemetery and sneak into the cornfield next to it for nighttime feeding sessions. He lifted one branch, so it didn't catch him in the throat and then made his way to the muddy—but tended—path. It would take a bit longer to get home using the path, but he couldn't think of any reason why he needed to rush to get home.

CHAPTER SIX

Business was always better when it seemed like people were getting along, thought Nick, while putting new pour spouts on a couple of new liquor bottles. The bar was empty, save for the evening bartender, who was in the basement grabbing new napkins and straws. George, who'd become as much of a friend as he was a patron over the years, had just left to get dinner at the Night's Quest. He'd been the only customer in the place for a half hour.

Hank's is a Mancheville stalwart. Nick knew it would take something crazy for it to fold—either severe mismanagement or something horrible. Not that he wanted that to happen, he'd never really viewed Hank's as competition. The owners even came to his bar, and he to theirs. But he knew that if one of the bars was going to fold, it was probably going to be his Mancheville Pub. He'd been talking to George about some of the business's struggles, although he'd downplayed the situation to avoid too depressing of a conversation. Even though he had the utmost trust that George would never run and gossip about the place and would be a great guy to open up to, Nick still thought George shouldn't have to listen to the pub owner cry about unpaid bills and unsuccessful investments while he drank his beer.

The truth was, the pub was definitely in trouble. It wasn't the first time it had ever been in rough shape. Running a bar or restaurant is a tough racket. Nick had always been very content with the space that the pub had filled in Mancheville. He loved that it was a place where people came early to shake off their workday and settle into the evening. He was happy to cooperate with the other establishments and take his fair share to support his family. There also used to be several folks that lived very close to the pub and never left for any other bar, but few did anymore.

Starting trivia and hiring some new bartenders were some new things that Nick was trying out to right the ship at the pub. His father had always been a proponent of changing things around when times were tough rather than just barrel on using the same tactics. Like the fancy speakers, he'd drive Nick's mother crazy with ideas and

schemes to drum up new business. The charm of his go-for-it attitude, and not necessarily his actual ideas, seemed always to inject new
life into the pub. Sales would enjoy a temporary burst to bolster the
business's health, and the family would have a little less pressure on
them.

Nick had certainly noticed divisiveness and resentfulness between
some of the customers. People were always going to go somewhere
to drink. Bars are imperfect places with many harsh realities to deal
with– alcoholism, criminal behavior, drug use, and sexual harass-
ment, to name a few. But a vibrant bar atmosphere can be a
welcoming place that feels safe and comfortable to many. That also
happened to be the most profitable environment and what Nick always strived to achieve. That was very difficult with the overbearing
rift between people politically and socially that left them uninterested
in, or vehemently against, conversing with those who had pissed
them off on a social media page—often when the activity was not
even explicitly directed at them.

Regardless, Nick would never throw in the towel until the bank
came and physically repossessed his towels and pint glasses. Nick just
couldn't blame shitty sales numbers on some kind of schism amongst
the townsfolk and use it as an excuse to sell the building before he
tried everything else in his power. The old man would be rolling in
his grave if that happened, Nick thought.

He grabbed George's empty glass from the bar and noticed that
he'd left a twenty and a five-dollar bill even though he'd only had
two cheap beers. The kind gesture brought a smile to Nick's face,
and he made a mental note to thank George when he saw him and
instruct the bartender to give him his first beer on the house the next
time he was in the pub.

George was finishing up his salad and crab cake entrée. Don,
Samuel, and Patrick had all eaten earlier at the get-together after Jim's
funeral. George was also there but hadn't been hungry. He never was
after a funeral service. Don, Samuel, and Patrick were now consuming drinks rapidly to celebrate Jim's life and drown their sorrows.
None of the four had been that close with Jim but had known him
well enough to attend his viewing and burial. That was enough of an
excuse to drink at double their regular rate.

"Shame about Jim," said Patrick with a sad headshake.

"Damn shame. He was a good, hardworking American," Samuel replied. He put a tulip bulb glass of brandy to his lips and let a half-ounce slide into his waiting mouth.

All four men were currently drinking brandy, as Patrick was pretty sure it had been Jim's favorite drink. He'd purchased the round, so nobody questioned his memory. The Night's Quest served the brandy in lavish snifters designed strictly for the liquor's proper consumption. The vessel held in the aromas and flavors until you took a sip. These snifters even had fancy etching on the fat, round bowl. They looked ostentatious and strange in the hands of the four men. But Patrick had insisted they use them and—more importantly—he had paid. So, they obliged.

George took his last bite of crab cake and chewed deliberately. He gently pushed his plate away from him and wiped his hands with his napkin after swallowing. With a thoughtful look on his face and his hands resting on his stomach, he took an ample breath, preparing to add his contribution to the Jim discussion. "Jim was always a very nice guy to me and Anna. I remember one time, decades ago, we bought a couch from him. Didn't ask for much money and even volunteered to deliver it. He knew we didn't have a truck that could hold it. We placed it in the living just how Anna wanted it. She changed her mind four or five times, and Jim waited patiently every time and followed her directions." George laughed with his eyes closed. "Oh boy, I was so mad at her. But I couldn't be angry for long when Jim was so nice and patient."

"I can't believe his health went south so fast in the hospital. They thought he was gonna be okay and maybe even able to return to work in a few weeks. Couple of days later, he's dead. They missed something, I guess." Don swirled his glass around and stared at the brown liquid dancing around inside. It had an orangey amber appearance when it crept up the sides, and the light showed through it.

Samuel finished his last sip before speaking. "I worked with him years ago at the foundry before it closed. He never missed a day of work the entire time I was there. He was as valuable as two men. He taught me a lot about fixing cars, too. He could have been a professional mechanic with his knowledge, but he said he never wanted to make his hobby into a profession. If I'd had half his knowledge about vehicles, I never would have set foot in that crazy foundry. I guess he knew what he wanted."

Patrick held his snifter up in a dramatic fashion. "We should have one more toast before we finish our drinks and head out."

The three others solemnly lifted their snifters and turned towards Patrick.

"Jim was strong in body and spirit, and we're all better off for knowing him. He was a fine example of what our little town can produce. He possessed many of the traits that we value, like concern for neighbors, getting done what needs doing, and passing on knowledge to the next generation. We hold his memory near and dear to our hearts. And—as the Irish say—until we meet again, may God hold you in the palm of his hand."

They clanked their glasses together as lightly as their drunkenness would let them. After everybody had downed what was left of their brandy, they sat, reflecting not only on Jim but also on their own aging and mortality. Each wondered silently what folks would say about them when they were dead.

Patrick gathered the ornate snifters and carried them towards the bartender who'd been standing respectfully at a distance, not interrupting their serious discussion. Before the bartender took the glasses, Patrick gave him a handshake and thanked him for going to the trouble of finding the snifters, cleaning them, and serving the brandy to them. Walking back to the others, he gestured with his head towards the door, and they all stood up and prepared to leave for Hank's.

Since it was the middle of summer, the sun was still hovering high above the horizon and putting off significant heat. The men walked in pairs with Don and George out in front of Samuel and Patrick. The healthy glasses of brandy had taken their toll on all of them, and they all walked like overgrown toddlers wobbling down the uneven sidewalks leading to Hank's. They'd started the short journey, all babbling back and forth but had settled into a several-minute quiet period.

Breaking the silence, George remarked, "My grandson will be visiting me in a couple of days. I love that damn kid."

"What's the occasion?"

"Nothing in particular. Sometimes he'll just visit so we can spend some time together, just the two of us."

Samuel seemed impressed and sincerely happy for George. "That's really great, George. My family lives two towns over, and I barely see them. Doesn't he live far away?"

"Yeah, pretty far. My daughter moved to Massachusetts over twenty years ago. Married her husband five years later and had Ethan. They're about an hour away from Boston."

"I bet that has been hard over the years, them being so far away."

"It has, but I usually see Ethan at least four times a year. Thanksgiving, Christmas, usually a visit in the spring, and at least one visit during the summer. I'm just happy that he ever wants to visit."

"Good for him. I met him once, and he seemed like a good kid—more than I can say for most others in his generation. Young people I meet are just so damn rude these days. Screwed up morals and shit."

George ignored his social commentary and shielded his eyes from the sun while looking forward and answered, "He's a great young man. His parents have done a great job raising him."

Samuel allowed several seconds of silence to pass, expecting more discussion about George's daughter and son-in-law. When no more came, Samuel pulled a cigarette out from his pack and a small black lighter from his pocket. He lit the end of the fresh cigarette, and George could smell just the slightest scent of bitter smoke touch his nostrils. Patrick put fire to his cigarette and took a substantial first puff.

No large houses or businesses were blocking out the sun for the last few blocks at all. Everything seemed to have a kind of warm hue, even the sidewalks, and streets. The flecks of fool's gold in the asphalt shone so brilliantly that it made the men rub their eyes when they caught a glance of them at a certain angle. The edges of the street signs sent off gaudy, colorful little rays of light that made the signs look like they were made of cubic zirconia.

A block away from Hank's, three children were playing a minimalist game of baseball. The largest seemed to be playing with the two smaller children. The tallest kept batting the ball with all his might and running the bases until one of the other two picked up the ball. He would shout out 'ghost runner' and return to whatever was serving as a home plate to hit again. With the sun enveloping them and the yard, it was difficult to tell if they were boys or girls, and they were young enough that their voices didn't make it clear. Finally, the tallest hit a pop fly that was caught for what must have been the third out. The two young ones traded places with the single before the men reached the backside of the Hank's building and couldn't see them anymore.

George and Don entered Hank's while Patrick and Samuel stayed outside to finish smoking their cigarettes. Megan hated when they came in with cigarettes dangling from their lips and took forever greeting people while ashes floated into the atmosphere inside. She much preferred they finished one before coming in, asked for an ashtray, and had a proper place ready to tap off the ashes of their next cigarette.

About once a quarter, Patrick makes it a point to bring up Don's 1986 Ford Mustang GT. Don bought it when it was only two years old with less than ten thousand miles on the odometer and had been driving it ever since. It was still his pride and joy thirty years after purchasing it. He still straddled lines in parking lots to take up two spots so nobody could park close to it. He washed and waxed it once a week, took it to Mustang club car shows, and still used it as his daily driver.

Even a car that's taken care of well is still vulnerable to aging. The clear coat was gone, so the paint job was somewhere between flat and glossy. The color was a bland burgundy with velour seats a half shade lighter than the outside paint. If you looked closely, there were bumps along the wheel wells where rust had taken over and been covered with touch-up paint by Don. The Ford badge on the car's nose was slightly faded and had some chips in the blue where stones had hit it. It was admirable that Don had kept a car running for over thirty years, but it was hardly an impressive machine anymore.

Don still saw the formidable, handsome machine that he'd purchased in 1988. That made it all the more delightful for Patrick to periodically poke fun at his Mustang and encourage him to buy a new car.

"Don, I think you have a hole in your exhaust, buddy. I heard you coming to pick me up to go to the gun range the other day, so I grabbed my gun case and waited outside. Seven minutes later, you arrived. That thing was howling so loud I could hear it across town!"

"That's called a V8 5.0-liter engine, Patrick. It makes more sound than that Japanese piece of shit you drive. That's the result of actually having horsepower."

"You had every dog in town barking!"

"You love to exaggerate about my damn car. I think you've been jealous of it since the day I bought it, to be honest."

"Not really my style, but it worked for you. It's had a good run, but I think it's time to retire it. You can afford something new. Maybe a Honda Civic, or a Prius, or something practical like that." Patrick sipped his whiskey with a fake look of innocence.

"My car will be American, it will make noise, and it will run entirely on gas. End of story."

"I've heard the Nissan Leaf is a great electric option."

"I'm gonna drive that damn Mustang till it falls apart. And when it does finally fall apart, I'm gonna leave it on your front lawn."

"I'll call the junkyard and let them know it'll be there next week."

Megan interrupted them and asked, "What do you want, Don?"

"I don't know if I can answer that; it might get me in trouble."

Without even acknowledging his inappropriate response, Megan changed her wording and asked firmly, "Would you like the same drink again, or would you like a different kind of alcoholic beverage?"

Don laughed it off like she was playfully flirting with him until he started to cough. When his cough subsided, he said, "Another of the same whiskey will be just fine, honey."

Megan pushed his glass with one hand, sliding it like a hockey puck to her other waiting hand. She held it up to the light and saw tiny bits of food where his lips had rested. There were also little patches of soap scale still on the bottom of the glass from the dishwasher. They were about the diameter of a pencil eraser and only visible when purposely placed in bright light, but it still wasn't great. Megan reminded herself to tell the owners to stop buying the cheap dishwasher detergent that always did that to the glasses. The soap scum wasn't Don's fault, but the food bits were. She guessed that he probably had soup at the Night's Quest and the little wet chunks were from the dozens of crackers that he always jammed into his bowl. They tended to hang onto his lip.

Across the bar, Alonso had recently sat down with Mo and Erin. He'd heard Don's response to Megan, rolled his eyes, and mumbled something behind his hand to the other two while gesturing with his head towards Don. A shot of some kind of clear liquor went down his throat, and he placed the empty glass near the edge of the bar, saying loudly, "Hey, can I get the beer that I ordered with my shot?"

Megan was still getting Don his drink on the other side of the bar. She didn't even respond to Alonso. The keg for the beer he'd asked for had kicked and was currently being changed over to a fresh one. Alonso must not have listened to her when she told him, or he had no idea that switching out a keg usually took more than two minutes.

When Megan delivered his drink, Don thanked her and then stood up on the rungs of his stool, peering over the top of her head. He looked squarely at Alonso and said in a raised, stern voice, "Maybe you can have a little respect when you talk to her. Not only are you yelling at her across the bar, but I also didn't hear you say please! You don't need to treat a woman like that!" He started to lower himself back to a sitting position but rose and added, "Asshole!"

An awkward silence fell over the place.

Alonso spit out, "You think she's worried about me?! You're the one hitting on a woman like forty years younger than you. Pretty sure I've seen you getting handsy with her before, too. I'm sure she's more worried about your creepy ass than me saying please and thank you!"

Megan was not having it. She knew all too well that squabbles fueled by drinks had to be handled immediately, or they'd accelerate. She hollered, "Both of you knock it off and mind your own business! If either of you says anything but an apology to the other, I won't serve you anything else!" She glared at each of them, moving her head back and forth a few times. She lowered her voice and said seriously, "I won't hesitate to cut you off."

Megan's firm regulation worked, and both Don and Alonso went back to speaking only with their own set of friends. A couple of people became uncomfortable and left, not wanting to be around if a larger confrontation broke out. They didn't need to. The room quieted to a peaceful murmur, and nothing else happened.

Hours later, George was the only person left in the bar. Megan was cleaning at a leisurely pace while talking to George. The last load was in the dishwasher, tables and bar were wiped down, and the area behind the bar had been swept. She'd even emptied all of the ice from the ice machine and sanitized it. Her last task was to bag up anything still usable from the garnish tray and throw away anything that wouldn't last until tomorrow. While she spoke to George, she casually wiped any liquor bottle that had wet or sticky residue on the side of it. They discussed the interaction between Don and Alonso.

"I mean, I'm not even worried about Don. I guess I should immediately shut him down when he says inappropriate shit to me, but I don't even really think about it anymore. I worry more about other female bartenders who might feel threatened or uncomfortable. He gets out of line, especially as he drinks more. I hate to say it, but it kinda comes with the territory to just let the flirting roll off your back if you're a women bartender. And as far as him getting handsy, that's not really a thing. Alonso likes to exaggerate sometimes. I think Don may have put his arm around my waist one time, and I yanked it off me so fast he got the message real quick that that shit doesn't fly."

George digested what Megan had said. "I guess he's always been a little too friendly with female bartenders. It's embarrassing when he gets that way. Honestly, I think he does it more out of some display of masculinity rather than thinking that it will ever end in a romantic encounter. He'd barely even know how to react if a bartender responded positively to his flirting. None of that makes it right; you shouldn't have to put up with any nonsense. He does have a special thing for you, though, I tell ya. He feels like he has to protect you like some damsel in distress at times."

"Exactly! The ridiculous thing is that it seems like everybody wants to protect me on their own terms and for their own purposes. Don tries to be some big protector guy when somebody doesn't treat me like a lady—whatever that means. I guess it means you can say vaguely sexual shit and do some unsolicited flirting as long as you're courteous when you ask for a drink. That old school mentality towards women is just so confusing to me." George just nodded. Megan glanced at the rag she was using to clean the bottles, wrinkled her nose in mild disgust, and tossed it into the trash. "At the same time, Alonso, and other guys like him, think they need to document everything creepy that Don does like they're building a court case against him. It feels almost as demeaning that Alonso thinks I'm so weak that he needs to speak up for me. I've never discussed how I feel about Don and his behavior. I guess I should appreciate his help, but he seems much more concerned with making himself look like a great, politically correct guy and Don like a piece of shit. It's like I'm just a tool for him to inflate his reputation as a good guy. A lot of self-righteous bullshit, really."

George smiled subtly and said, "I think you're pretty spot on with both of them. It's funny because I think they both have the same general frustrations and lack of self-confidence deep down. They just act out in different ways because of those things. That's all I can say; I don't want to speak for either of them. They both have plenty to say on their own."

George and Megan both laughed. They both responded to a noise at the front door, with Megan taking her elbows off the bar and George sitting upright in his stool and turning his head. It turned out to just be a gust of wind. They both relaxed again.

"I also don't want to speak for other women. I can only talk about this stuff from my perspective. I just know that in most situations, I can take care of myself. I'm not arrogant, and I'm not saying I never need help. But I like people to respect me enough that they allow me the chance to handle things on my own first. Maybe that's why my last boyfriend was a guy that never did anything for me. I made more money than him. I defended myself constantly with shitheads while bartending in New York City, even while he was sitting at the bar watching it all go down. Hell, I even kicked a guy in the junk one time who was trying to mug us. It worked too; the guy turned and ran as fast as he could with serious pain in his guts and nuts. I always wondered—if push came to shove—if my ex could help me in a terrible situation."

"And that is the guy you had your son with, is that right?"

"Yep, that's him. He's not a horrible guy, and he helps as much as he can with our little guy, Logan. I don't ask for much from him. It didn't take too long to realize that we weren't meant to be, but we were together long enough for me to get knocked up. His sperm was the most ambitious part of him, unfortunately. I wouldn't change it, though. I'm very happy here in Mancheville with Logan."

George took a very long pause before speaking, not quite sure if he wanted to say what was on his mind. He did anyway. "Forgive me if I'm being too personal, but did you always plan to have the baby? With all that doubt about your relationship's future, I have to think you were at least a little scared about bringing a child into the world. Again, I don't mean to be inappropriate with my question."

"No offense taken. Believe me; it crossed my mind. But I realized I wasn't in that bad of a place. I'd saved some money while bartending. It can be pretty lucrative if you get in the right places and don't get too involved in the lifestyle of drinking, which I didn't. I have a decent relationship with my parents. They're not wealthy, by any means, but they provide something of a safety net if anything goes wrong. And I was in my late twenties when I had him. I would have been terrified if I got pregnant when I was nineteen or something. So, I concluded that I could handle having a kid. It's been tough at times, as it is for anybody, but wonderful overall. He's my dude."

George noticed how late it was and took his final sip of beer. "I do love the pictures you post of you and Logan on BrainSpot. It's a highlight amongst a lot of trash. You guys seem to have so much fun together. Logan reminds me a lot of my grandson when he was the same age. But anyway, I'll get out of your hair so you can close up for the night. It was nice talking to you, Megan; appreciate you sticking around and chatting. Good night."

Megan was already at the light switch and turned off all the lights once George opened the front door. From the darkness, she responded, "Same to you, George. You're one of the good ones. I've seen enough bad ones to know. Good night to you."

George had an oddly strong sense of her congenial smile even though it was pitch black. He exited before his old confused emotions made him weep at her kind words, but he left the door open, so there was enough streetlight for her to find her way out.

CHAPTER SEVEN

There are some behaviors that George, being a bit on in years, purposely avoids so as not to become the stereotype of an old man. Driving slowly is not one of them. The more he aged, the less he cared about getting places in a hurry, and the less he cared about other drivers getting angry with him for going slow. George's opinion was that if you have to rush to get where you're going, you probably didn't plan properly. Or you're too busy for your own good. He always drove around the speed limit and never purposely slowed down to piss anybody off, but he also didn't alter his speed to accommodate anybody's dangerous driving. Retiring had only given him more time and one less place to go in a rush.

Another thing that signaled his age was that he still paid all of his bills by paper and still wrote some of his friends by hand. Rarely, but he did it. Despite being sufficiently skilled at using a computer, he liked to prepare his bills on paper and drive to the post office to mail them. The process made it easier to remember which ones he'd already paid. Making it a monthly routine that he physically had to act out was better than just clicking a button.

He'd gone to the Top Star Hardware Store to buy a new watering can for Anna's plants that he still maintained. In addition to amaryllis, she had a fondness for orchids and peonies. She'd also kept numerous potted plants on their screened-in porch. He still watered several rubber tree plants, snake plants, coleus, and a variety of herbs. He didn't eat any of the herbs anymore, but he still liked how they looked. Plus, he felt like he had an obligation to keep every plant alive when Anna passed. Maybe it was because he had often remarked that it was a little silly to have so many potted plants stashed on their porch. Keeping the plants alive felt like some kind of penance.

He'd talked to John at the lumber desk at the hardware store for an hour about nothing in particular. Maybe some Phillies talk. Possibly a discussion about their grandchildren. And there was always the weather when they couldn't think of anything else to say. George had gotten lumber a few times for small projects and went to the hardware store enough to have struck something of a friendship. A classic older man acquaintance where the talking was easy, and they could speak for hours without sharing anything very personal.

After the hardware store, he'd gone to the post office before heading back towards his house. He had to visit the grocery store later, but he wanted to spend a few hours at home first. A lime green Volkswagen GTI had been behind him since he turned out of the little plaza where the post office was located, along with a small art gallery, craft beer store, consignment shop, and Chinese restaurant. The GTI started riding on George's bumper immediately and hadn't let up for miles. At one point, the car had even honked at him and moved their arm in a circular 'hurry up' motion. George didn't deviate from driving the speed limit and had only gotten annoyed enough to mumble, "Jeez, get off my ass already."

Once home, George booted up his computer and went to the kitchen to brew a pot of coffee. He scooped out coffee from a large plastic container without counting how many. Another thing about Anna, he remembered, after taking several heaping scoops without really paying attention, was her insistence on using exactly three and a half scoops of coffee when making a pot. She'd let George start scooping, but after three, she'd immediately remind him only to add another half to the coffeemaker. Then she'd remind him to fill the pot with water to the eight-cup line. No more, no less. This made coffee that was much weaker than George would have preferred, but he didn't care enough to argue. It was still coffee. If she weren't around, he'd fill the pot with water until it felt about the right weight, then load up the filter until it was three-quarters packed with coffee. Now she was never around, so he went through a lot more coffee than the two of them ever had. Thinking about it reminded him that he needed to buy coffee at the store later.

With his steaming cup of coffee in hand, he sat at his computer and logged in to the backend of his blog. There were no comments, not even spam to delete, and nothing needed to be updated, so he closed that browser window and logged on to his social media. He didn't care if he was the only one in the house; he never let any programs or websites allow him to stay logged in. It just felt more secure. Remembering a different password for everything he used daily was another attempt to keep his brain sharp.

Scanning social media entertained but also aggravated George. Several people he knew from the bar scene had a BrainSpot account, and about half of them used it regularly. George had a BrainSpot page, but he mostly used it to see his daughter's pictures, post links to his blog posts, and spy on other people. Not spy in any kind of malicious way. He just liked to see what people were up to. There were plenty of differing opinions among the people he knew about just about everything. Politics, religion, and current events being some of the biggies, of course. BrainSpot seemed to be where most people heedlessly dumped their opinions and passive-aggressively shared controversial videos and articles, both proclaiming their feelings while also safely distancing themselves from the content because they didn't create it.

In many ways, the BrainSpot feed didn't change that much from day-to-day. George would scroll through the most recent posts and shares to find any new pictures or videos from close friends or family members. He skipped anything that was just complaining or venting. Megan often posted pictures of her son playing sports or playing on the playground. Sometimes positive updates about school or well-behaved evenings at the babysitter. George admired the graceful way that Megan used BrainSpot. He had honestly never seen her engage in an argument or share something remotely controversial. He couldn't even recall her posting anything but a massive amount of pictures of her son and a couple of goofy selfies.

Earlier in the morning, Megan had taken a bunch of pictures of her son behind a miniature drum kit and posted them to BrainSpot. George clicked the 'approve' button on a shot of the kid with a massive grin on his face and his stubby arms held up high with a white-knuckle grip on a pair of drumsticks. The 'approve' button seemed a little silly to George. It was a little illustration of a pink brain with two cartoony eyes and a broad smile. He felt kind of absurd, clicking the thing to artificially show his approval, but he did like encouraging pleasant contributions to BrainSpot.

Moving on, he 'approved' his cousin's retirement announcement, several beautiful shots from a former coworker's trip to the Grand Canyon, an action shot from his favorite Phillies player Bryce Harper, and a post from the Mancheville Community Page about newly installed swings and basketball hoops at the town park.

Another post that caught his attention was some pictures and a video of a model train. They were posted by a friend who now lived somewhere on the west coast. Either Washington or Oregon, George couldn't remember offhand. Kenneth Dickerson was his name. They had only been acquaintances. Anna had known his wife from grade school, and they had a monthly tea date. The couples had also gone for dinner for a period and played a Tuesday night bridge game together. Now, both of their wives had passed, and Kenneth had ramped up his collecting of model trains.

He had an amazing assortment of train sets that George estimated to be in the tens of thousands of dollars. George had no knowledge of model trains whatsoever, but he'd started casually researching the shrunken engines, cars, and cabooses when Kenneth started upload-ing pictures of them to BrainSpot. They were quite impressive. He even had amazingly detailed layouts that complemented the trains themselves–brick-walled factories, quaint homes, exquisitely compli-cated steel bridges, delicate fashioned flora and fauna, and yard after yard of functioning train tracks.

Browsing through the train pictures, George remembered a trip that he'd taken when he was about seven or eight from Philadelphia to Chicago. It was the longest journey he'd traveled by train in his entire life. That was not the only reason that it was memorable. A few hours into the trip, a disagreement near the front of their car had grown from a verbal quarrel into a shouting match and had finally erupted into a full-on brawl between two men.

It was hard for anybody on the car to make heads or tails of what exactly had caused it. From what people were gathering, things had been tense from the get-go because the one guy's huge trunk was encroaching on the space that the other guy had on the overhead rack for his bag and briefcase. Only glares, and snorts, and long ex-asperated exhales, were exchanged at first. By a half-hour in, their anger was dulled, and they both were able to concentrate on reading the newspaper.

Some passengers thought the comment that sparked the disagree-ment was about a football team from the sports pages, while others insisted they had clashing views about a story from the politics page. Whatever it was, it resulted in the two middle-aged men grunting and grabbing and throwing poorly-aimed punches while others tried to clutch their arms and disengage the fighting pair. The few robust punches that landed had a strange thudding sound that terrified George. It was nothing like the funny whap sound that he'd heard in movies. And seeing two grown men completely out of control was an incredibly upsetting occurrence for him.

Watching the tussle upset George greatly, and it took at least an hour of consoling from his mother before he calmed down enough to leave her arms and return to his seat with a picture book. He'd never liked conflict. He'd been pressured into a few fights as a child before developing enough confidence to simply exercise his passive nature and walk away from physical confrontation. He'd had three fistfights, to be exact. Somehow—and very narrowly—he'd been the victor of two of them and carried a winning record. But, win or lose, he always had the same reaction afterward to run sobbing home to his mother's soothing presence. She pitied him so much she couldn't even bear to punish him. She'd silently run a bath and let him rest in the hot, steaming water until his tears stopped, and he could speak again without his voice quivering into unintelligible gibberish.

Thinking about that train ride and the fight still made George uncomfortable, so he clicked the 'approve' button on the video and quickly scrolled down to make the trains disappear.

As was typical, both Alonso and Don had been very active on BrainSpot since George had last logged on to his page. In the sea of negative BrainSpot posts, Don and Alonso were easily the most prolific who showed up on George's feed. They were similar in the activity level but dissimilar with the nature of their posts and shares. George despised a large percentage of what both of them posted, but he was still drawn to read and scrutinize it.

Don had felt compelled to share various things since George had last looked at the feed. All of them, George noticed, had been 'approved' by Samuel Squire. Most of them, only by Samuel Squire.

The first article he'd shared about a homeowner husband and wife being forced to remove the American flag from their property. George had seen several iterations of this kind of article. It was typically an American flag, or something military-related, or maybe even a cross. The headline of the article would only say that the homeowner had been forced to remove the item. If you clicked on it, buried in the article was the detail that it had nothing to do with persecuting the people for religious purposes or out of some anti-American spite. It was nearly always because the item broke a rule of the homeowners association to which they'd agreed to abide. George read this article, and that was exactly the case.

Of course, the nature of the rule was to prevent large, gaudy displays and tacky yards that might hurt the property value of the surrounding houses and the neighborhood in general. It also removed the possibility that neighbors would fly flags that were somehow opposed to each other and cause a conflict. Articles like the one Don had shared twisted the story to make it seem like the people were targeted unfairly. Having to remove an American flag was stupid, but they had signed a legal document that disallowed flying any flags on their front property.

George had always hated the idea of an HOA. He would never live in a place where somebody told him what to do with the property that he had purchased with his money. And on top of that, pay them regular dues to do so. But it was silly to live in an area with an HOA and then expect to be exempt from the rules. In addition to HOAs, George also hated divisive articles that created a false sentiment that patriotism and Christianity were under great attack. That's not to say it never happened, but to manufacture anger by manipulating a situation through a crappy article was not the way to combat real problems.

The second thing that George came across on the BrainSpot feed–approved by Don–was an image of the Republican president praying. He had a peaceful look on his face, and his hands were resting in a relaxed fashion against his stomach with his fingers interlaced. A bible was visible on a podium in front of him. The bright red, bold text on the picture read:

'LIBERALS ARE DEMANDING THIS IMAGE BE REMOVED FROM BRAINSPOT. SHARE AND LIKE TO DEFEAT THEM!'

George had seen things like this before–several times from Don. There was plenty of venom towards the president and probably many people who didn't like looking at the picture. But the commentary on the picture was just a trick to get people to engage with the post and widen its reach. It was another kind of shameless and divisive type of post that frustrated George.

Not to be outdone, Alonso had his fair share of mildly repugnant BrainSpot behavior. It wouldn't take a stranger long to look at Alonso's BrainSpot page and figure out that he was a passionate atheist. George wasn't sure of what exactly his upbringing was. Indifferent agnostics and reasonable atheists generally don't say a damn word about how they feel on the subject unless asked about it. Sometimes, not even then. Intense atheists often have some deep-seated bitterness about religion that foments a need to demean others' faith. George wasn't exactly sure how or why he'd gotten there, but Alonso was definitely the latter.

On his BrainSpot feed, George saw something that Alonso had left on a Christian BrainSpot page named 'Living Biblical Truth Fellowship' that had a picture of a cross with a lamb lying beside it as the main image. Alonso had replied to a comment in which a BrainSpot user had pasted the following Bible verse:

Let the peace of Christ rule in your hearts, since as members of one body, you were called to peace. And be thankful. Colossians 3:15.

Alonso responded:

Peace my ass! All you Christian Republican dicks throw praises to your magic daddy in the sky while you treat poor people like shit, tolerate racism, and let pastors and priests rape kids! Religion and spirituality are just something fools hide behind because they can't think for themselves!"

Even in his seventies, George had not come to any firm conclusions about God and spirituality. Anna had gone to a couple of different churches over the years with some regularity. George had attended with her a few times. Nothing had ever spoken to him, but it took no effort to be quiet and let people have their own experience. He recognized that religion could be perverted and used to manipulate people. He considered it un-American to allow any single religion to seep into policies that were supposed to represent all people. He despised religion being used to justify prejudice.

Despite some of his misgivings about religion and faith, it still depressed George to see a young person so angry that he needed to abuse others on a page devoted to their religious beliefs. From what George could see, the 'Living Biblical Truth Fellowship' BrainSpot page made no mention of politics or anything inflammatory. It only posted magnificent nature scenes, inspirational quotes, and Bible verses. Regardless of his spiritual status, George was saddened to think that a person, especially a young person, seemed so resolved to give up on any kind of faith whatsoever.

Alonso had shared other posts with headlines like: "G.O.P. is the new Nazi party," "Doctor claims president in final stages of fatal illness," and "MLB Rookie of the Year favorite apologizes for racist middle school tweet." At least a dozen more hyperbolic or emotionally charged posts from Alonso peppered the BrainSpot feed.

Just scanning Don and Alonso's obsessive posting, sharing, and approving was enough to tire out George. He finally stopped scrolling and logged out of BrainSpot and his computer. He still had some shopping to get done.

George glanced at the list he'd made for the grocery store. His goal was usually to have everything in his cart and be in line or checking out in twenty minutes or less. Because he ate pretty simply at home and often had meals at the Night's Quest or a local diner, George rarely had to buy much food on a grocery store trip.

This afternoon trip was a pretty standard one for him. Milk and eggs. Lunchmeat and a loaf of bread. Cans of condensed soup. Plastic-wrapped Styrofoam rectangles with meat on them; one with pork chops and a one with chicken breasts. Giant can of coffee. A container of salt with a twist top allowing the salt to be sprinkled sparsely or poured in a steady, open stream. Bag of fun-size candy bars. Microwave-ready bags of frozen vegetables, including broccoli and green beans. Four expensive apples that were perfectly crisp when you bit into them.

He'd have been done in sixteen minutes if he hadn't forgotten the coffee and had to return to an aisle through which he'd already been. Still, seventeen minutes and thirty-eight seconds wasn't too shabby. On his way to one of the three cashier stations with a light on, he heard somebody call out his name. He was caught off guard for a moment and swung his head back and forth several times before seeing Mo and Erin. Mo carried a full basket in his left hand and a two-liter of soda in his other hand. Erin held a gallon of tea in each hand, the weight of them dragging down her slight frame. They greeted him and joined him in line nine.

"I'll ask him. It's worth a shot," Erin said, her shoulder shrug abbreviated by the cumbersome plastic containers.

"Ask me what?"

Erin turned her attention to George. "Hey, this might sound kind of weird, but would you be interested in buying two tickets to a concert tomorrow night? It's a band called Portugal. The Man. Indie rock stuff."

George answered with a confused look on his face, "Pour the what?"

Mo and Erin laughed before she responded, "Portugal, like the country. The, like the. Man, as in a grown-up boy. It's a silly-ass name, I know. They're pretty dope, and they put on a good show, though."

George nodded like he knew what she was talking about but silently wondered if the band name meant something that his old age prevented him from knowing.

"We wouldn't normally ask somebody your age if they wanted to go—no offense—but you always seem to like all different kinds of music at the bar. It'll be Mo, me, and Alonso going. Alonso's brother and his girlfriend bailed on us at the last minute. We want to at least get back half the money for the tickets, so we don't get totally screwed. We figured we'd offer them to you since we saw you. Interested?"

It was funny; George was a little stung by the age comment but flattered that they offered the tickets to him. Even so, he was about to decline since he knew nothing about the band. Then he remembered that Ethan was coming into town. Ethan is a music nut, and George was confident that he'd at least know who they were. It would be a fun thing to do with his grandson, and he had to admit that he'd enjoy getting credit for taking him to a show that was—as Erin put it—"dope."

"How much are you looking to get for the two tickets?"

Mo replied, "They're sixty-five each face value, but we'll sell you both for the price of one."

"I'll tell you what. I'll call my grandson, who'll be visiting me tomorrow. If he likes the band and wants to see them, I'll give you a hundred for the pair to help you out."

"Oh, that would be awesome!" said Mo with a smile.

"I'll check out, and then I'll call Ethan while you're checking out. If he wants to go, I'll get cash from the ATM for you."

"Sounds great!"

Mo and Erin watched George unloading his groceries while engaging in small talk with the cashier. Once his transaction was finished, he pushed his bag-filled cart beside the water fountain, out of the way of anybody passing. He used his index finger to navigate his phone screen and found his grandson's number after a few taps. George held the phone up to his ear and turned towards the wall, examining the store managers' portraits. Mo and Erin could hear him talking, although it was slightly muffled since he was still facing the wall.

They placed their items on the belt. Erin greeted the cashier and said, "He's a pretty nice old dude. He's friends with that Don asshole, but he's pretty cool himself."

"Yeah, for sure. He's always been nice to me. His friends seem a little freaked out by me because my real name is Muhammed. I thought Don's head was gonna explode when somebody at Hank's told him that was my full name. Probably thinks I'm a terrorist." He was kidding, but honestly wasn't completely convinced Don didn't think that.

Erin giggled while swiping her debit card and punching in her pin. "Maybe he'd like you better if he knew your parents vote Republican and go to a Lutheran church."

"I wouldn't want him to get his hopes up that he and I are gonna be friends."

They grabbed their purchased items and stood near George, waiting for him to finish the call. When he did, he turned to them with a pleased look on his face.

"Good news! Turns out, Ethan loves that band and is really excited to see them! Just let me get some cash for you, and we can work out the details of where and when we'll meet tomorrow."

CHAPTER EIGHT

"I'll be there in about ten or fifteen minutes, Grandpa. I just got off the exit."

"That's great; glad you got an early start." Ethan had only driven from his college, not Massachusetts, but his school was still two hours away and a lengthy drive. He was taking a summer course while working at some seasonal warehouse job. George was proud of him for getting ahead in his schoolwork. The computer science program he was in was pretty rigorous. The only way most graduated in four years with a decent G.P.A. was to take some summer courses to lighten the regular semesters' load.

"Yeah, me too. I need some coffee, though. Should I stop? Do you want any?"

"If it's okay with you, just wait until you get here. We'll go to the diner and get breakfast. I'll be ready to go right away and have the car started.

"I can definitely wait; that sounds like a good idea. I didn't eat anything this morning."

"Okay, Ethan. See you in a little bit. Drive carefully."

"I will. Bye."

"Bye."

George ended the phone call and returned to rocking gently on his front porch chair and drinking his coffee. Despite already sweating, he still liked to drink hot coffee outside sometimes. He'd even heard before that drinking a hot drink on a hot day can cool down your body temperature but wasn't sure if that was an old wives' tale or based on science. Staring at the two bushes in the landscape bed near his mailbox, he tried to remember where he'd heard the thing about the hot drink cooling your body.

Before he knew it, he'd pondered long enough that Ethan arrived and pulled slowly into the driveway. He hadn't even gone to grab his keys.

Ethan waved and shouted with a smile from the driveway, "I thought you were gonna be all ready to go! You're not even in the car yet!"

"Even worse, I didn't go back in to get my keys. Just wait out here; I'll be right out."

George quickly returned from inside the house, bopped down the porch steps spryly, and walked down the paved path in the front yard towards the driveway. He and Ethan embraced warmly, both patting each other's back like they were burping each other. They let go, and both hopped into George's Ford Explorer.

Every time George passed the department store, he had a strange feeling. It had been in decline for years, but George still remembered when the entire town was excited as hell that it was opening. Some weren't happy about it, as they saw it as a threat to the smaller businesses in town. They weren't entirely wrong, but it hadn't been quite the retail apocalypse that some had predicted. It was one of those odd things about growing old that George hadn't gotten used to. Watching stores and restaurants and hair salons go through entire arcs of existence didn't make him feel like a wise old man; it just made him feel old.

"Is that place still in business?!"

It was like Ethan had read his mind.

"Somehow. I think it's one of the last of that chain in the country. I can barely go in there anymore without feeling depressed at how bad it's become. Because of that, I rarely do."

"Too easy to buy online."

"That's certainly the way it's going. I don't buy much on the Internet, but plenty of people I know buy just about everything online. I guess you can't judge things off of me; I don't buy much at all. I buy new clothes every couple of years when they wear out. I buy screws, duct tape, and plant food at the hardware store. I go to the grocery store for food. That's mostly it, really."

"Have you bought anything online?"

"I bought a bulk pack of underwear because I was sent an email offer that I couldn't refuse. Got a bag of coffee that was supposed to be amazing but turned out to be crap," George thought for a little bit and added, "And I won that old Phillies pennant I have in an auction."

Ethan laughed at his short list. "I think mom usually buys more stuff in one week than you've purchased in the entire time you've been using the Internet. She loves getting packages on the doorstep, and she hates going out to shop."

"She wasn't always that way about going shopping. Of course, that was probably more of an excuse to hang out with friends and sneak cigarettes at the mall."

Ethan laughed again at the thought of his mother being a mischievous teenager.

George swung into the diner parking lot and found a parking spot near the front of the building.

After ordering and receiving Ethan's pancakes, his omelet, and two fresh cups of coffee, George asked how things were going for Ethan.

"It's been going pretty well. Mostly just working and going to class a couple of times a week in the evenings. It's a pretty basic programming class. Some of it is review from high school and stuff I learned on my own, but I'm learning some new stuff too. It's not bad."

"And the job?" George lifted a bite of egg and waited for his answer.

"That's good too. It's just a lot of lifting and packing stuff. Mindless, for the most part, but it's a nice change of pace from going to class and having to concentrate on a bunch of code and logic. It sucks sometimes, but there are days where it's kind of a relief to not think much, get some simple tasks done, and go home. No disrespect to the full-time people; the job gets more complicated the longer you're there. They give the really easy boxes to seasonal people like me, so that's why it's mindless for me."

George enjoyed Ethan's humility immensely. "I'm glad you appreciate all different kinds of work. Believe me; you get a lot more people on your side if you approach everybody with an attitude that what they're doing is important to your success."

"I know," Ethan paused and added with a smile, "Although I know I don't want to pack car parts into boxes the rest of my life."

"And there's nothing wrong with knowing that. That's why you give different jobs a shot when you're young; it gives you the motivation to figure out what you really want to do. I worked a bunch of different positions at the paper mill before somebody gave me the opportunity to take some information systems classes. Before ya knew it, I was one of just a couple of guys maintaining the entire plant's system and keeping everything operating. I enjoyed it most days."

They both cleared their plates, and George paid the bill.

They weren't sure what they wanted to do until Ethan suggested that they go bowling. George hadn't been to the alley since Ethan was just a little kid, but he was up for throwing a couple of games. George was pretty impressed with his bowling, considering how long it had been since he'd rolled a ball. He bowled a 127 and a 133; about as good as he used to score when he at least went a few times a year. Ethan surprised him by bowling a 155 and a 171.

George realized that it was silly to think that he'd still be able to beat Ethan like he was a child, but he at least thought it would be close. After Ethan kidded him for a few minutes after the game, he admitted that his college had a special night on Wednesdays where students bowled for free, and he'd attended every single night. He'd gotten much better from the regular practice, so it wasn't a fair fight. George was simultaneously proud and mildly annoyed at Ethan beating him.

George was not exactly feeling like a young whippersnapper between thinking about the department store and losing to Ethan at bowling.

They both sat at the table behind their lane with their rented bowling shoes sitting in front of them. Ethan sucked from the straw protruding from his Styrofoam soda cup. It was absurdly large for the small cup. The straw was designed for the giant slushies that they also served at the snack bar. They had shorter straws that were more appropriate for the petite soda cups. George had a bit of a flashback and realized that Ethan had always selected the giant straw when he got a soda at the bowling alley. It was at least ten years since they'd been to the alley together, but George distinctly remembered the long, bright red straws always poking out from Ethan's cups.

"So, tell me again, how did you come across these tickets? It's sick you got them, but it's kinda random."

"There are a few college-age kids that I always see at the bars around town. I'm kind of friendly with everyone. Alonso, Mo, and Erin are the three that I see the most. They're only a couple years older than you, so you might even know them."

Ethan thought for a moment but shook his from side to side and said, "Doesn't sound familiar. I only know a few people from Mancheville."

"Anyway, I saw Mo and Erin at the grocery store. They're dating, by the way. Alonso is their really good friend. Alonso's brother and girlfriend were supposed to go to the concert, but they had to back out at the last minute. So, Mo and Erin were looking to get some money back quickly on the tickets that they'd already purchased for those two. They saw me at the store and mentioned the tickets to me. I called you to see if you knew the band. When you said you liked them, I bought them."

"That's awesome. Will we meet them at the concert?"

"They're general admission tickets, so we're not in assigned seats. They're very friendly, though. I imagine we'll plan to arrive around the same time at the venue and hang out together. It's called Stage AE in Pittsburgh. Hour and a half drive. Alonso can be a piece of work at times, but he should be fine tonight unless he finds somebody to argue politics or religion with."

"Oh, one of those guys, huh. I read it enough online. I hope I don't have to hear it during the concert."

"Exactly. You remember my friend Don, right? He and Alonso are always at each other's throats about one thing or the other. They post stuff on BrainSpot and get all angry with each other before they even come to the bar. Then, they start putting drinks into the mix, and all of a sudden, they're pissed off at each other. They aren't the only ones, but they're two of the worst in town."

"Half the stuff on BrainSpot is pure crap anyway. People just post the craziest stuff they find, and it gets popular because they want it to be true. They'll share or approve anything that supports what they already think is right. My friend and I created this fake website for a class where we made up bogus political articles. We started with something true but then spun it in some crazy direction that would make people go nuts. We even started a BrainSpot page where we shared our articles and some videos and memes from other political pages. The page got almost a thousand fans in less than two weeks without doing much except creating fake articles and sharing other people's content. We started getting some pretty scary emails from intense people, so we shut it all down before it got too weird or dangerous."

"Wow, I guess I never really thought about just how easy it is to create pages like that. No wonder there is so much crap floating around."

"I'll show you the BrainSpot page when we get back to your house. It's still around; it's just not live to other users anymore."

"I'd like to see that. It's funny, but it's also kind of scary."

"Oh, definitely. We were even able to choose an anonymous setting so we could manage the page without anybody knowing it was us. Lots of people that make political pages don't care at all about what they're posting; they just drive traffic and try to make money from ads and stuff. Although, you don't make a lot of money unless you commit to it like it's a full-time job."

"We'll check it out later. Do you ever play pool? We can shoot a few games while we're here."

"Are you just looking for something that you know you can beat me at?"

George shrugged in mock innocence and said, "I don't know what you're talking about."

"I hardly ever play, but I'll let you win a couple of games," Ethan said with a smile.

George did win all three games they played. Two games of eight-ball and one round of nine-ball. It wasn't close in any game, but Ethan was a good sport about it. He even tried to pay for their table time at the front desk, but George never let him pay for anything.

After leaving the bowling alley, they decided to hit the Night's Quest for a sandwich before they went back to George's house. By the time they made it back, they were both in need of a nap if they expected to make it through the concert later. George went to his bed and collapsed on top of the covers without removing his clothes or sneakers. Ethan plopped down on the couch in the living room and turned on a rerun of some old sitcom that put him to sleep in less than two minutes.

George woke up a little later than he had hoped, but they'd both still have time to get quick showers and change before leaving for the concert. Even a little bit of time out in the brutal heat just going from George's SUV into the bowling alley and restaurants had been enough to leave a layer of sweat and accompanying grime. George figured it would be nice to have a refreshing shower before leaving for the concert.

Ethan was still sleeping peacefully on the couch with the television droning another episode of the same sitcom. George decided to let him sleep a bit more and made his way to the bathroom to get his shower first. He peeled off his clothes and threw them in the hamper in the corner. He glanced at himself briefly in the mirror above the sink, grabbing the paunch around his waist that held a smattering of gray and white hairs. He shook it a bit to see how much it rolled and jiggled. The results didn't exactly make him happy, but he countered to himself that many men his age were much worse off in terms of a belly. He flicked on the lights above the sink to give himself more light in the shower.

He stood under the hot water contemplating if it was stupid for him to attend a concert of some band that he didn't know where he might be the oldest person in the audience. He wasn't trying to relive his youth or pass himself off as hip. He truly just thought Ethan would enjoy himself. He rinsed the shampoo from his hair, and it occurred to him that people who still used the word 'hip' were almost definitely not hip. When he finished rinsing, he heard Ethan moving around in the living room and kitchen.

George emerged from his bedroom, fully dressed in jeans and a light blue Phillies t-shirt with the classic maroon 'P' on the front. Ethan was sitting at his desk and had George type in his log-in password to use the computer. Once in, Ethan opened the browser and logged in to his own BrainSpot account. He brought up the inactive political page that they'd discussed earlier and left it open for George to view, then stood up to go get his quick shower.

George perused the BrainSpot page and marveled at the interactions with the content on the page. It was all dated to some extent, so some of the articles and videos were about topics that were no longer relevant, which made it seem all the more absurd that people were losing their minds and typing such nasty comments and replies. They insulted other commenters, typed multiple paragraph rants to nobody in particular, and posted crass images of politicians they hated with snarky captions and unflattering edits. George had seen similar pages before, but it just seemed more shocking knowing that Ethan and his friend were the ones operating this one. George closed everything on the screen and shut his computer down. He went to the kitchen and grabbed two twenty-ounce bottles of Coke from the refrigerator in preparation for the ride to the concert.

Ethan always enjoyed going on long trips on Pennsylvania roads. He was fond of the mixture of farmland and forest that one could view when driving through Pennsylvania's rural sections. The roads themselves were pretty terrible other than the Turnpike. Anything not on the Turnpike was often pockmarked and full of potholes and rough strips where the road was patched instead of completely repaired. Ethan noticed it, but his grandfather seemed oblivious to the subpar asphalt. Of course, it always took a lot more than trivial things to get him excited or angry. Ethan, off the top of his head, couldn't even remember a single time where he could say his grandfather was sincerely pissed off.

They'd been moving along on the shitty roads leading out of Mancheville for about fifteen or twenty minutes. They passed a green state-supplied sign with white lettering announcing the next town—West Petersburg—and a '1' to designate it was only a mile away. Ethan had spent a lot of time visiting his grandparents over the years, but he was only vaguely familiar with the town. He'd forgotten about it until seeing the name on the road sign. He never came into Mancheville from this side, when visiting.

Ethan wondered if it was better to live in one of these towns that didn't attract much attention than to reside in cultural centers like New York or Boston, or L.A. or San Francisco on the West Coast where everything seemed to be happening. He often thought about where he would like to live after graduation. He bounced back and forth between wanting privacy and isolation versus having immediate access to everything, if he lived in a city. It was a fairly common conflict, Ethan knew, for many people his age. Even with three years of college left, he couldn't help but feel pressured to make some firm decisions about his path in the future. It seemed that just as many of his older friends were returning to their parents' homes after college as were striking out on their own. Some were just not cut out for it and never should have wasted their time in college. A few had the brains for success at a university but were lazy or unmotivated. Most struggled with debt and had a difficult time finding a place to start their career. Not an unfamiliar story, a problem that plagued even well-meaning students. Ethan was doing his best to leave college with some kind of direction, at least. He'd even considered offering to pay his grandfather some rent to live with him for a few years once school was over. It wouldn't be a full jump into adulthood, but it would at least be something different than moving back home full-time. It might help him get his footing in the real world, and his grandfather would probably love it. Living with a grandparent might

not be appealing for most fresh college graduates, but most of them
didn't have a grandparent that not only scored tickets to a bad-ass
indie rock concert but also went along to see the show.

A quarter-mile beyond the road sign, Ethan noticed a billboard
for a place called Romaine's. Ethan squinted at the slogan towards
the bottom of the sign but couldn't quite make it out. He read it out
loud, murmuring, "When in. When in what?" Ethan looked at his
grandfather, but he was either concentrating on the road, was day-
dreaming, or his age had started to affect his hearing. Ethan carefully
uncapped his bottle of Coke, making sure the carbonated liquid
didn't rush out and end up on his lap or the seat. He took a quick sip
and then returned for a long swig before spinning the cap back on
the top. He adjusted his seat to a comfortable, laid-back position that
still allowed him to view the scenery.

After another half hour of driving, George interrupted the silence
by stating, "We're meeting the other three at the front gate at Stage
AE to all go in at the same time. Alonso has the tickets on his phone,
so he'll get us scanned in. Shooting for 6:30; we should be good if
parking isn't hard to find. They sent me a text with all that info. I
was able to read it, but I can't drive and text. Can you just answer
them for me? Say 'sounds great, see ya then' or something like that.

"No problem. What's your password?"

"6499"

"Hey, my birthday!" Ethan typed in the password and answered
the text in a flurry of thumb movement. "Done." He put the phone
back into the cup holder where it had been.

Less than an hour later, they were parked in a garage, had met the
others at the front gate, and had their ticket barcodes scanned.
They'd found good spots near the center of the crowd that was building. Maybe fifty or sixty yards out from the front of the stage. After
the bustle of parking and getting through security, they were all enjoying standing around casually listening to the opening act, which
was one guy playing chill electronic music on a loop station, synthesizer, electronic drum set, drum machine, and various other smaller
pedals and devices. They all seemed happy to breathe a bit and relax,
and George and Ethan finally had the opportunity to greet the three
friends properly.

"Alonso, this is my grandson Ethan. Ethan, Alonso. Can't remember if you two ever met."

Alonso shot Ethan a friendly grin, and they slapped palms in a low five. "I don't think so. You've talked about him at Hank's before, but I don't think we've ever actually met."

"And this is Mo and Erin, who were nice enough to catch me at the store and offer the tickets."

Mo and Erin both gave friendly waves, and Ethan gave a pleasant nod to both of them.

"Thanks, guys; I can't believe it worked out that my grandfather got us tickets to see Portugal. The Man when I'm visiting him!"

Alonso laughed and said, "George is pretty damn cool. He's one of the older guys at the bar that we get along with. Not sure about some of his buddies, but George is always nice to us," He changed his focus to George and went on, "That Don guy hates me, I swear. Course, I'm not too fond of him either. He's freakin' gross with the bartenders, and he seems pretty racist. Just the other day, there was a black dude at Hank's, and Don couldn't stop staring at him. He just can't stand anything different from other old white guys. I think you were there, George."

He had no idea what Alonso was talking about at first. The nights at Hank's tended to run together in George's mind, as much from old age as from inebriation. He thought for a moment, and it came back to him. "Oh, he was just trying to figure out if he was the pro at this golf course he played at before. He wasn't sure if any of us recognized him or not. I promise it had nothing to do with him being black."

Not totally convincingly, Alonso said, "If you say so. I trust you. I still don't like that dickhead."

"Well, for what it's worth, I've been friends with him for decades, and I've never heard him be blatantly racist or use any racial slurs. Don is far from perfect, but he might not be as bad as you think if you had a chance to talk to him. I certainly don't love everything about him, but he is my friend."

Ethan, Mo, and Erin all had awkward smiles on their faces listening to the two discussing Don.

Alonso sensed he was a little too forward about Don, so he let George have the last word about it.

Mo clapped his hands loudly and said in an exaggeratedly excited voice, "Okay, let's just drop that subject. How about that opening band guy, huh? Dope-ass music, right?"

They all laughed and relaxed again. Which, for the four people under thirty, meant immediately pulling their phones out to browse their social media, or text a friend about the concert, or whatever it is they did when they had their heads bowed to their phones. George didn't get upset about it like some people his age. He accepted that he wouldn't completely understand their relationship with phones since he didn't grow up with them like Ethan and the others. Still, he couldn't quite wrap his head around the idea that all four of them were comfortable standing together while each person is engrossed in something completely unrelated to the others. It didn't seem healthy, but George was more confused by it than upset. For all he knew, they were texting each other, and he was entirely out of the loop. They had all traded phone numbers with Ethan already. Regardless, it didn't seem quite important enough to point out to anybody. George even mindlessly checked his phone several times in less than three minutes, subtly mimicking their behavior without even thinking about what he was doing.

When the next song was over, George offered to buy everybody a drink if somebody would go along and help him carry everything back. Erin and Ethan both said they wouldn't mind waiting with him in the beer and soda line. Alonso and Mo stayed back to save as much room in their spot as possible, dancing playfully and bobbing their heads to the booming music.

As it turned out, they made it through the drink line reasonably quickly and were back right as the opening act was finishing his last song. They all touched their cups together for a quick 'cheers.' George and Erin were driving afterward, so they both decided to just drink sodas instead of start drinking alcohol. Ethan had an iced tea since he was too young to drink legally. He would have considered just sneaking it, but they were using OVER 21 bracelets, and he'd already seen a security guard pouring out a beer from the hands of a young lady who didn't have a bracelet.

The lights went out, and the area was almost completely pitch black. There were only a couple of small lights for the crew on the stage's sides and the red and green LEDs on the amps and speakers. The crowd immediately erupted into screams and shouts in anticipation of the band appearing. It occurred to George that it had easily been at least twenty years since he'd packed into a general admission area for a rock concert. He and Anna had gone to plenty of concerts, but the last couple of decades were shows where they paid for comfortable seats where they could view the show without getting tired or sweat on by other concertgoers. It both excited and worried him, but mostly excited him.

George was surprised at the relatively small stature of the mustache-bearing lead singer when he came out on stage and provoked a resounding roar from the crowd. His diminutive frame seemed even smaller because the pants he wore rolled halfway up his calf. He also donned a cream-colored bucket hat that rode so low on his forehead that you could just barely make out the wireframe glasses that sat high on his nose.

The stage was still dark except for a few red lights that pierced the darkness, giving off just enough glow to see that all band members were now on stage. George wasn't exactly sure what to expect from the music, but he certainly didn't guess that their opening song would be a pounding instrumental cover of a Metallica song. They ripped through a few minutes of the song, complete with wailing guitars, crashing cymbals, and even the ominous bonging bells. He'd never been much of a heavy metal fan, but he was familiar with the song and remembered the name when he heard the bells.

They immediately moved from the heavy tune into a series of tamer but no less spirited alternative rock songs with guitars, heavy bass, and a smattering of bending and beeping sounds from the keyboard and synthesizer. The crowd would wiggle and groove through funky, psychedelic sections and then hone in on the guitarists when they wailed out fast, frenetic solos. From what George was hearing, the band's signature was the high-pitched falsetto that the lead singer used in pretty much every song. His ability to maintain a clear, unwavering pitch while singing way up in the stratosphere was awe-inspiring.

They surprised George again by throwing in an abbreviated cover of Pink Floyd's Another Brick in the Wall that was surrounded by two of their original songs. He had never been a musician, so any time a band conceived interesting medleys with several songs mashed together, it always blew him away that they could connect it all seamlessly.

At one point in between songs, Alonso reached down into his calf-length sock the whole way into his sneaker. He pulled out a slender pen-looking device and waved it in front of Mo happily. He cleaned the end off with the tail of his shirt, stuck it into his mouth, and sucked heartily on it for about six seconds. He let out an ugly cough while passing the pen to Mo. He took a healthy dose of his own, just barely shorter than Alonso's. He held out the pen to Erin, who declined to take her hit but passed it onto Ethan. He inhaled for a few seconds before releasing the button on the pen. Removing it from his lips, he offered it to George with a grin. George knew it would probably delight them if he took a hit of what he deduced was potent marijuana juice, and he was intrigued by the weird little instrument that he'd never seen before. But he'd always been a drinker only, so he had no idea how he would react to the stuff. He waved away the pen with an amused smile.

After a second act of extended jams and quieter songs that highlighted the singer's voice and had lyrics that the crowd frequently sang along to, the band banged out a heavy rock song, and the stage darkened with the audience still shouting and demanding an encore. They came back out and played one last cover: their take on the Beatles' Hey Jude. George recognized their final original song as it had been in a host of commercials. He wasn't entirely sure, but he gathered from the lyrics that it was called *Feel it Still*. The song had the crowd going bonkers with its infectious bassline and slick groove. George was giddy feeling Ethan's shoulders bump his own while he oscillated left to right, wore a massive grin, and seemed utterly captivated by the music.

In the parking garage after the show, they were all saying goodbye before separating for two different vehicles when Alonso asked, "So what did you think, George? Did you like Portugal. The Man?"

"I really did. It was a little weird but in a good way. I'm not sure about the lead singer's wader pants and Gilligan hat, but those guys are definitely talented. I think I liked just about every song they played."

Mo laughed and said, "That's good to hear, George. You have good taste. It's seriously so cool you brought Ethan to the concert. Thanks for buying the tickets."

"Thanks, Mo. I appreciate you guys offering them to an old fella like me."

"Yeah, George. We're glad somebody could use the tickets after my dumbass brother and girlfriend bailed on us."

"What happened with them, anyway?"

"Eh, it's kind of a long story. Let's just say my brother isn't exactly known for being reliable. But anyway, glad you and Ethan made it to the concert."

"Dude, I had a blast. That band is so tight." Ethan said exuberantly. He hadn't stopped smiling and dancing since they'd left the venue. "Thanks, Grandpa. And thanks for offering him the tickets, guys!"

They all exchanged a final salutation and departed for the vehicles.

CHAPTER NINE

Almost everybody at Hank's started murmuring around the same time. It must have looked strange to the few folks who still didn't use a smartphone. In a matter of minutes, nearly everybody staring at a phone became extra concerned about something on their screens.

The 'something' was either a news article, social media post, text message, or some other electronic alert about a robbery at a bar in West Petersburg called Romaine's Restaurant and Lounge—frequently shortened to just Rome. Once the shortened name caught on, customers started shouting 'When in Rome!' any time things got crazy or weird late at night. It became their official slogan; it was even on the billboard they paid for on the edge of town. And it wasn't uncommon for things to get crazy or weird, so the bar frequently lived up to the ambiguous promise of excitement. In this case, the customers would have preferred a boring night.

West Petersburg was only five or six miles south of Mancheville, so it was close enough to be shocking for the Mancheville residents. The restrained murmurs and moans developed into full-blown disturbed exclamations, head shakes, and concerned conversations with barstool neighbors. Everybody in the bar had been to Romaine's at least once. Nearly every drinker in the local area went to Romaine's for their famous 'Night Befourth' party. It started at dusk on the third of July and was one hell of an extravaganza that left everybody hungover at their picnics the next day.

The reports said that there were three known suspects. The offenders had worn ski masks, so their faces hadn't been identified. There did seem to be agreement amongst those at Romaine's that the trio consisted of two men with large builds and one woman of medium stature. One of the men was fat, and the other one was muscular. The woman appeared to be fit and had large breasts that were perky enough to be fake. The breasts were not reported in the news, but everybody at Romaine's mentioned them as identifying characteristics to the police officers.

Her breasts had also been the way she'd caught the cook off-guard and locked down the kitchen. When he finally stopped stirring and turned around from his pot of soup, a pair of bare breasts was less than six feet from his face. He was so surprised that he dropped his wooden spoon and left a splatter of reddish-brown broth on the cement floor. She pulled her shirt down to cover herself and used his bewilderment as an opportunity to put her gloved hand over his mouth. She quickly pulled that hand away and stuffed a sock into his mouth with her other hand. She pulled a roll of duct tape from a fanny pack and quickly wrapped his head enough times to stifle his yells but not cut off the air supply to his nose.

She kicked at the back of his legs, not hard, but strategically placed so that his legs buckled. It wasn't difficult as he was probably in his sixties and wasn't in great shape. She wound the duct tape a dozen times around his wrists and ripped it with her teeth. Pushing his face towards the floor, she stuck a knee into his spine and wrapped his legs together about twice as much as she had his arms. She secured the bolt lock on the door leading out to the bar so nobody could run into the kitchen. She also locked the door that opened to the parking lot. With everything secure, she ran into the tiny office that was barely larger than a broom closet.

The flashing and duct tape wrapping had been done in less than forty-five seconds, and the cook was so shocked that he never fought back. He also never got a thorough look at her breasts, so his description to the police ended up being so vague it wasn't usable. Besides, nobody in the sheriff's office was even really sure how they would go about inspecting suspects to find a match. It would be extremely tricky, and to make it more difficult, West Petersburg didn't even have a female officer.

The female thief made it to the parking lot with five zippered deposit bags that would have been delivered to the bank the next day if they hadn't been stolen.

While the woman had been taking care of the kitchen, her two partners had entered the bar area after making sure nobody was in the parking lot. They'd quickly and quietly entered the bar with pistols drawn, two for each man. They immediately collected everyone's phone. Only one man talked, speaking firmly but not shouting when he gave directions. There were only six customers and a bartender at the bar, so it wasn't too much for two armed men to handle. All complied without argument and dropped their phones into the paper grocery bag that the silent masked man carried around the bar.

The man giving directions was silent until he saw the last phone dropped into the bag. After that, he demanded keys from the bartender to lock both of the doors so nobody could enter and surprise them in the middle of their robbery. The bartender grabbed nervously at the ring of keys hanging on a belt loop on her cut-off jean shorts. After a few tries, she finally unclipped the keys, separated the bar key from the rest, and handed them to the robber who spoke.

He moved slowly toward the front door, not taking his eyes off the customers. A couple was sitting near the front door, and he used the gun to direct them to move to the other side of the bar where the rest of the customers were sitting. The wife let out a small cry while she and her husband walked carefully towards the others. Both had their hands up even though nobody had told them to do so. They dropped their hands and sat down silently when they came to the two stools closest to the other customers and the bartender. The robber who spoke locked the front and side door, then returned to the front door where he stood with both guns still drawn.

The silent robber moved to one of the few small tables in what passed for a dining room near the bar. He set the bag of phones on the table. With one of his guns still pointed towards the customers, he slid his other gun into a holster on his waist. He took each phone out of the bag, one at a time, and turned each one off before laying it face up on the table. He pulled his second gun from its holster and used the butt to smash each phone's screen until all of them were unusable. He returned the gun to his holster and walked briskly to the landline phone sitting beside the cash register. He ripped out the cord from the base of the phone and casually cut it in half with a pair of scissors from a cup on the other side of the register.

The silent robber, still beside the cash register with one drawn gun, used a gloved index finger to summon the bartender. She raised both hands and jolted up, knocking over her stool by accident, which hit the floor with a loud bang. Two customers ducked, one covered her face, another screamed, and the couple embraced while simultaneously shouting, "Oh my god!"

When the bartender started to reach for the stool, the robber at the front door said sternly, "Leave it!"

The silent robber again summoned the bartender, and this time she made it to the cash register without causing a disturbance.

Again, the robber at the front door spoke up and said simply, "Open it for him, then move a few steps away from it."

She tapped a few keys on the register, and it opened with a click and a dinging bell sound. She obediently took three steps away from it. The wordless robber used his empty hand to unzip the fanny pack on his waist. He began stuffing bills from the register into the pack until the tray was empty. It couldn't have been more than a few hundred dollars, but the cash register money was not the most important prize sought after by the robbers.

The huge 'Night Befourth' party had occurred the previous weekend, and the trio of criminals knew that the real treasure would be found in the bank bags in the office. All of the cash collected from the annual Independence Day bash. The only time of the year it would be worth it to rob this mostly insignificant small-town bar. They lived an hour from West Petersburg and had stumbled upon the previous year's 'Night Befourth' on a drunken whim. One of them pointed out that it was a cash-only bar and thousands of people attended the giant party. They'd hatched the robbery idea while getting drunker and drunker and watching the community fireworks from their truck tailgate in the parking lot of Romaine's.

They mostly considered the idea a joke until they visited Romaine's again the week after the 'Night Befourth' party. While they sat at the bar drinking light beer, the kitchen door swung out and was held open by the cook. The bar manager, a fiftyish woman, emerged from the tiny office with an armful of zippered bank bags stuffed full of cash and exited the kitchen. They all stared at the woman before turning to each other with enormous grins. They laughed, and each took a long pull from their bottle of beer. After that, they visited the bar periodically to watch the employee's and customers' behaviors so they could start seriously planning their heist.

The two male robbers continued to hold the customers and bartender at gunpoint. Neither said a word, and they seemed to be waiting for something. Moments later, a knock in an unusual pattern came from the front door. The robber with the keys unlocked the door and tossed the keyring to the back of the dining room. They dashed out the door and slammed it shut. In seconds, a roar of an engine and squealing tires could be heard from inside the bar. The husband ran to the front door and yanked it open, but the vehicle was already far enough down the road that he couldn't identify it from the diminishing red taillights.

The robbery took place at Romaine's around 8:30. Hank's customers started getting news of the incident less than two hours later.

CHAPTER TEN

Hank's was buzzing with excitement and anxiety about the robbery that had occurred just a few miles away. Folks were throwing out names of people who they thought might have done it. Theories arose, suggesting it was an inside job. Somebody said they knew a bartender and a cook who were fired pretty close together, and maybe they had recruited a third person and decided to rob the place. Megan passed out drinks throughout all of the excitement, allowing the volume to rise higher and higher as long as nobody was arguing with each other.

That, of course, did not last long.

Samuel lamented to nobody in particular, "I don't know what the hell is going on in the world. Robberies and shootings and shit. All the damn time. Why can't we go back to when things were simpler?"

Mo only occasionally participated in tense barroom discussions, but he felt compelled to respond to Samuel. "So, I guess nothing bad ever happened when you were younger? What happened at Romaine's sucks, but it's not like robbery is this brand-new thing."

Samuel didn't even look towards Mo but remarked loudly, "The country is going to shit, and if you can't see that, I don't know how to help you."

Before Mo could say anything, Alonso chimed in, "If the country is in trouble, it's because of your greedy-ass generation raping the next one. Nothing is affordable for anybody except rich old white dudes anymore."

Samuel rolled his eyes and shot back, "Why bring race into it? Nobody said anything about anybody's color or race. You hate white people even though you are white!"

"No, I'm just comfortable being around people who might look different than me," Alonso said with a look towards Mo.

Mo was not a fan of having his Middle Eastern ethnicity pointed out, even if it was subtle, so he immediately looked regretful that he'd engaged Samuel and gotten the whole thing started.

Megan shouted, "Guys!" She was placing clean new pint glasses upside down under the bar on a rubber mat and stopped to cry out the one-word warning.

The tone went back to a more conversational one, and they went back to discussing Romaine's.

Patrick was something of an expert about all of the drinking establishments within a three-county radius, so he could always weigh in on bar discussions. It didn't mean he was always right, or even often right, but he was happy to give his two cents. "Rome has been mismanaged since the new staff came in five years ago. They shoulda just let Barney keep running it!"

Gene, the eldest of Mancheville's two mail carriers, was seated at the bar with a dark beer. "Barney let half his friends drink for free and nearly ran the place into the ground before they fired him," he retorted.

Patrick gave Gene a big dumb grin and said, "I know! I was one of those friends. That's why I was mad; they fired him!"

Gene snorted in amusement and returned to his dark beer. There was a smattering of laughter, and the room relaxed a little bit more.

When George arrived at Hank's, it was nearly midnight. He noticed that Alonso, Mo, and Erin were already seated at the bar. Ethan had gotten a text from a friend who lived within walking distance of George's house. He'd developed a friendship with him as a child when he visited his grandparents but didn't often get to see him. The friend was having a party and invited Ethan over after the concert. He'd left not long after they arrived home. George had considered just staying in, but he was awake because of his afternoon nap, so he'd ventured to Hank's. He wasn't aware that he'd be walking into a beehive of frenzied activity.

George purposely walked near Alonso, Mo, and Erin so he could greet them.

"Hey, guys! Glad to see you made it back safely from the concert!"

Erin responded, "Yeah, we made good time getting back home. Even with that small detour in West Petersburg."

"Same with Ethan and me. There wasn't any traffic or anything else to hold us up."

"Did you hear what caused the detour in West Petersburg?" asked Mo.

"Can't say I did."

"There was a robbery at that bar called Romaine's. They shut the road down while they were investigating the bar. Here, check out the news story on my phone."

He handed his phone over and let George read the article to learn the details of the incident. George scrolled with his index through the story. He went back to the top and slowly scrolled down again while rereading the story before handing the phone back to Mo.

George shook his head and said soberly, "Wow, that's crazy. Must have been scary as hell for the people at the bar; can't imagine something like that happening at Hank's. Glad nobody was hurt. Thanks for showing me the article."

"No problem. Isn't that nuts! It's all anybody has been talking about in here."

George nodded and began making his way around the bar towards where Don, Samuel, and Patrick were sitting. They greeted him, and he sat down on the empty stool next to Don. Patrick and Samuel were both smoking their cigarettes with an extra sense of stimulated energy, not even bothering to put them in the ashtray in between draws. They didn't seem to notice the little flurries of ash that would periodically float down onto the bar. Megan would see later when she went to wipe the surface with her bar rag.

George settled onto his stool and tried to pick up the gist of their current conversation. It didn't take long to realize that they were throwing out guesses as to how much money the criminals had stolen from Rome's.

"I'll bet they got over fifteen grand," offered Samuel.

Patrick scoffed at the guess and said, "After that big fourth of July blowout they throw, you think they only have fifteen grand in cash? You forget they're a cash-only bar? They might have fifteen grand on a normal week. Wouldn't surprise me a bit if they doubled that. Maybe even more."

"Oh yeah, I forgot that they only take cash there; they're one of the few that still do that. You're probably right; they probably made off with thirty easy," Samuel said agreeably.

Don had been thinking. "I've heard they've gotten fewer and fewer people for that. There were a couple of arrests last year, and I think people are a little spooked that the police are watching it too close. I'll bet it's over twenty, but not much more."

Patrick conceded with his facial expression that Don might be right. "Who knows. We'll have to wait to hear the amount on the news. Far as I know, they haven't talked about that at all yet."

Samuel took a massive gulp of beer and shook his head. "Bastards should be shot. It's a damn shame nobody in the bar had a gun on them. Bartender must not have even had anything to protect herself. Back in the day, they'd have had a .38 hidden near the register. Assholes wouldn't have gotten a penny!"

Samuel had again attracted Alonso's attention across the bar. He whined loudly to Mo, "I just don't get it with some people, how the answer is always to have more guns. There's a goddamn robbery, and the solution is that everybody at the bar should have had a gun and had a big shootout. I swear, the stupidity is astounding sometimes."

Samuel's face got red, and he dashed out his cigarette vigorously. "Some people, known as liberals, will just sit like cowards and let themselves be pushed around. After all, they'll just wait for the next government check that they didn't earn. They'd rather watch innocent people suffer than put themselves at risk."

Alonso no longer pretended to speak to Mo or Erin. His voice went higher and louder while crying out, "And gun-nuts are so trigger happy that they're desperately waiting for their opportunity to put a bullet into somebody because they're unhappy about other shit in their pathetic lives. These psychos have some dream of being a hero, and they're willing to make dangerous situations even worse because of that!"

Surprisingly, Don had said nothing so far, despite usually being the first to jump into a verbal tussle. He more than made up for his brief period of silence when he spilled out, "That robbery in West Petersburg just shows you that there are evil people out there, and I refuse to sit back and just let them get away with it. I'll tell everybody right now, not being specific or anything, but they wouldn't get far if something like that happened here. The robbers, I mean. We have a God-given right to protect ourselves, and I won't hesitate to use it." He was sweating profusely, both from the temperature in the bar and his intensity.

Don wiped his temples with either arm and continued, "Megan, you better believe nobody is gonna come in here and steal from this place, and they sure as hell won't be threatening you with guns or anything else without being stopped. If it has to be me that does the stopping, I'll do it."

Megan looked uncomfortable at his words but didn't stop him from speaking—afraid how he might take it if she interrupted his diatribe.

"I don't need to flash anything around, but you better believe that I have the means to take care of business if anything happens to my friends or family. And it's always ready. My point-of-view is that I'll take the situation into my own hands and worry about explaining self-defense later. I don't need to wait for the police, and I don't think a business should have to let thieves steal from them and wait for reimbursement from insurance to get back on their feet."

Samuel stared in silent reverence for his friend, while Alonso glared wordlessly in a state of uncertainty, fear, and contempt.

After admiring Don, Samuel jumped in, adding, "Us good people need our guns. If ya outlaw guns, only outlaws will have guns!"

The cliché took much of the air out of Don's passionate speech and reminded those who knew him that he'd likely never fired a gun at anything more menacing than a deer or a paper target.

Alonso glanced at Mo and said, "Oh, jeez. I never knew how safe we were in here. Thank god we have these real Americans to protect us!"

Samuel hollered back, "You say that like a smartass, but you don't know how right you are. And you take it for granted, just like our freedoms as Americans!"

George, silent through everything, had not even made it halfway through his first drink. He did something that he rarely ever did. Some call it an 'Irish goodbye.' He could no longer bear to listen to the arguing and petty back-and-forth in the bar, so he left enough cash to cover his only drink and exited the bar out the side door without saying anything to anybody. The sweltering air outside was even more unpleasant than the thick air inside, but the silence was a great relief.

CHAPTER ELEVEN

Ethan had gone back to college after eating the scrambled eggs and pancakes that George made for breakfast. Before eating, they'd sat at the computer, and Ethan had shown him some of the projects that he was currently working on for school, as well as some from the previous semester. Most of the work was way over George's head in the technical sense, but he loved seeing the result of Ethan's intelligence and skill. Even when Ethan described things that were way too complicated for him, just because it was fun to hear him rattle off the programming and coding lingo that was now second nature to him.

They also looked again at the fake political pages that Ethan and his friend had created. In one sense funny, in another sad, George was still fascinated at the ease in which somebody could create a page that people passionately interacted with, as long as the slightest bit of effort was made to create a professional-looking design layout. The number of users questioning the site's legitimacy was vastly outnumbered by people who didn't care who created the content. George moved back and forth between the computer and the stove while cooking the eggs and pancakes. Ethan showed him some ways that he and his friend made the site look more credible and the places where they linked stories and pulled videos from to build up their content. George let one of the pancakes burn on one side because he was so intrigued, listening to Ethan.

But now, Ethan was gone, and George had a full belly that left him not wanting to get up from his computer. He still had most of his coffee left, so he sipped it while looking at the ten-day forecast. Hot, hot, hot as hell, hot, hotter, not horribly hot, hot, hot as hell again, scorching hot, and hot. Hopefully, the guys arranged their next round of golf on that day when it wouldn't be horribly hot. He closed the weather website and logged into his BrainSpot account.

George wasn't surprised at how his BrainSpot feed looked after the arguments at Hank's the previous night. Gun-related posts weren't the only thing on it, but they vastly dominated any other content. Both rabidly pro-gun and passionately anti-gun. From the usual suspects and their supporters. It was like a chaotic boxing match with opponents trading wild haymakers with little concern for where exactly they're aiming.

From Don came a story about a grandmother shooting two would-be thieves who broke into her home. They were unarmed, but Edith had started keeping a .38 Special in her nightstand since her husband had passed away from cancer seven years prior. The two uninvited men had been sneaking around her home, and Edith was only startled awake by the urgent barking of her corgi. Edith was able to slightly open her door and put two bullets in the back of one of the men and a single bullet in the other's neck. The story came with a convenient link to the NRA's website's landing page, where you could join the organization. Samuel Squire had clicked his approval on the story on Don's page.

Alonso shared an image of two cute young boys, both about six or seven years old. They had goofy grins, both wore the same baseball uniform, and each had an arm around the other boy. The first line of the caption had eight yellow sad face illustrations with tears streaming from the eyes. Below the picture, there was a paragraph of text explaining that the boy on the left had gotten his hands on his father's gun when the case it was stored in had been left unlocked. He was playing with the handgun and had mistakenly shot his best friend in the stomach. He died a week before he was supposed to start second grade. The text was accompanied by a link to a petition that you could sign demanding gun control be instituted immediately to end such accidents. It was only the ambiguous concept of gun control, and there was no mention of any specific legislation, but it did have over 3,500 signatures already. Erin left a comment that both she and Mo had signed the petition. Alonso approved the comment.

Next was a gaudy graphic with blasts of red, white, and blue streaks backing the figure of a skeleton with a .44 Magnum pointed with a perspective that made it look like you were looking into the business end of the large weapon. Bright green letters circling the skeleton spelled out, "You can take it… from my cold, dead fingers!" In the corner was the name of the group that had created it, the Gun Patriots of America. T-shirts with the graphic were on sale for $22.00 in the comments below the picture. George saw the image twice in his feed because Samuel had also shared it on his page.

Checkmate. Flicksake. Cliptake. The word was on the tip of George's tongue, but he couldn't for the life of him remember the term that Ethan had used. The article's title proclaimed: We Could Have Stopped Every Mass Shooting in History and We Chose Not To. He didn't need Ethan to teach him not to click on articles with such outlandish titles. The tactic angered George every time he saw it used, regardless of what position the article was taking. Alonso was a serial sharer of pieces with such ridiculous titles that one had to be almost delusional to think they had legitimate answers to anything or any reasonable points to make. Clickbait—that was the word. It came to George from out of nowhere. That's what Ethan called those articles.

Of course, it was unlikely that Don and Alonso and their respective crews were trading the content back and forth in direct response to each other. More than likely, they were logging on at sporadic times and clicking and posting and approving things, each in their little vacuum.

George scanned a few more posts before logging out and standing up deliberately to avoid tweaking his back. He was successful, but there was a variety of cracking and popping in his legs that accompanied his rise from the chair. After everything in his body seemed settled, he padded off to his room to grab his sneakers. He would walk to the cemetery to spend some time with Anna and purposely take a long and leisurely walk to get there. Realistically, few physical activities could be described as leisurely at his age, as evidenced by the percussive pops and gristly grinding of his bones and joints just from standing up after sitting for more than five minutes. Still, he'd found pleasure in planning out a walking route that took him past the quaint grocery store that he only used to grab milk or toilet paper (they couldn't compete with the massive chain one near the edge of town where he'd seen Mo and Erin). He planned to go by the Lutheran church, the 55+ community with a spectacular garden and lanky sunflowers, a playground where Ethan had once broken his nose falling off some monkey bars, and end up at the neatly manicured cemetery that held Anna's headstone.

He tugged a sneaker on each foot while resting his behind on the round arm of the couch. It was a compromise between completely sitting, which might retighten his body, and standing while bending over at the waist, causing his belly fat to squish his lungs and result in lightheadedness from lack of air. He tightened both sneakers carefully with a double knot. He stood up on his heels a few times as if to test the athletic shoes for functionality. He grabbed a bottle of water from the kitchen, as well as a square foot of aluminum foil. From the porch, he chose a lily to put on Anna's grave, wrapping the severed base with the foil to preserve its life a little longer and provide him something to grip the flower without damaging it while walking.

CHAPTER TWELVE

The lily was already starting to wither by the time George reached the cemetery. He'd stopped at the water fountain in the park and let some water flow into the top of the aluminum foil surrounding the poor flower, but it didn't seem to help it at all. George thought maybe the headstone's shadow would give the flower some relief and help it retain some beauty for a couple more days. Perhaps the little bit of hydration would eventually absorb into it and add another day.

Today, George decided to go through several rows of headstones on his way there. He saw the name of an acquaintance that used to frequent The Mancheville Pub. They'd shared little more than a few drinks and the occasional buzzed conversation. He saw a name or two that he thought he recognized from his youth, friends of his parents or shopkeepers or teachers. He started trying to find people who had been his age or close to his age. It so happened that the row he was in held all people who'd been born well before him. George felt oddly comforted by it. For fun, he started counting how many plots he could pass before he reached someone who would have been his age or younger, if not deceased. After reaching five, he began to feel selfish and silly and realized that if he was looking for some kind of evidence that he was young, it probably meant that he was, in fact, kind of old.

Despite the drooping, George still gently laid the lily in the lush grass in front of Anna's headstone. Whereas he'd silently reflected when he last visited Anna, today, he felt compelled to speak out loud. There was nobody else in the cemetery, so he wasn't restrained or embarrassed about having an audible one-way conversation.

"Hi, Anna. Not sure if you're there. Wherever 'there' is. Or what it is. Perhaps it's so exciting you don't have time to listen to me talk about my boring life on Earth. Maybe you're nowhere, and I'm just talking to myself to feel a little consolation and solace. Maybe you're somewhere, and you're already seeing everything that's happening and already knowing all of my thoughts and feelings. However it is, I'll still say that I love you and I miss you and I think about you all the time. How can I not with all of those plants I have to water?

"I've felt such a mixture of happiness and frustration in the last week. When Ethan visits, I'm so grateful and proud, and it's all I can do to not just say it to him the entire time he stays. That would make him uncomfortable, of course, so I just enjoy it. We went bowling like we used to when he was younger—probably been a decade since we last went. Had some nice relaxing, casual meals and got to talk about what's happening in his life. He seems to be doing very well with school, which isn't surprising. He's so damn smart; I can't get over it.

"I'm sure he's working hard too, but all of the computer and technical stuff just seems to come so naturally to him. With his smarts and how nice of a kid he is, I honestly think he can do just about anything he wants to do. It sounds like such an unoriginal thing, like a Hallmark card you give to a high school graduate, but I really feel that. I guess I'm just biased because I'm his grandpa. But we went to this rock show with these young people I know from Mancheville, and he was able to talk with them like they were old friends. He's so wise, especially for his age, and he has an understanding of people and life that took me decades longer even to begin to process. All I seem to hear about from my friends is how horrible people his age are, and I wish they all could just sit and have a conversation with Ethan and maybe have their minds changed.

"Speaking of that, it's been tough to be around the crowd at Hank's and the other bars. It has gotten so bad with the tension about politics and cultural stuff that people argue about. They read and watch so many things created for the sole purpose of preying on emotion and knee-jerk response to get views. And for what? To sell ad space and get people to buy things. You know me, and I don't hate technology or people making money. But there's just something unnatural and strange about so much of what people are consuming.

"Lots of people are creating their feeling of self by what they do online, allowing others to curate an environment and feed it to them while they slowly adopt it as their identity. Instead, they should be using the technology to advance and evolve what they already know of their true self. They're losing it. It's especially rough with relationships between younger and older people, from what I see almost daily. Maybe it's just history repeating itself, but it does seem a little bit more than that.

"Ethan showed me these pages he made online where he and a friend were able to completely manipulate people into reading and reacting to their page just because it had all of this stuff that got people worried, or angry, or confused. All mental states that nobody should be in when interacting with strangers who have no context for their lives or personal histories. Honestly, I've thought about creating my own pages on social media just to experience what it's like to post things and see people lose their minds. Maybe a little personal challenge to see if I can get people to pay attention to my pages. A page each from both ends of the political spectrum, just to make it even more interesting. I don't know if I want to be involved with it all, but damn would that be entertaining!"

George laughed at the thought. Not because it was impossible, it would be an interesting little social experiment. More because he was standing alone in a cemetery with his voice steadily rising in volume while he discussed it with, to any onlooker, just the muggy air and the small clouds of gnats floating around his head. Maybe that was enough talking to Anna for today. George smiled, sure that Anna would agree.

He gave a long last glance at Anna's headstone, tracing her name, the two dates, and the decorative ivy chiseled into the granite. He made a mental note to bring a towel or rag and give the headstone a quick cleaning sometime in the next couple of months. He scanned down to the ground. It was probably his imagination, but the lily seemed to look slightly more revived and refreshed.

CHAPTER THIRTEEN
ONE MONTH LATER

Many buildings in Mancheville had been built with bricks from a long-gone brick manufacturer that once operated in the town. Most of the brick houses have had several dozen coats of paint applied to them, while the buildings used for business and commerce had naked bricks on their exteriors. The raw brick buildings more obviously show their wear and tear, with visible chunks and cracks. With the painted brick, one might not even know some are brick until you walk right up and view them within a couple of feet. When you get closer, the slight difference between various coats is apparent where some of the paint chipped off, and you can see where the painted bricks had also succumbed to weather and abuse. Some cracks had gotten so wide that paint could no longer sufficiently fill them.

Most of the buildings near the town center were extended rectangles with symmetrical windows and slightly overhanging roofs. They're handsome but not ornate. Some were very old and even protected as historic buildings that couldn't be torn down or altered in certain ways. There's an old log building nestled in amongst the taller structures near the post office. It was once a blacksmith shop, then a furniture maker, and finally a post office. When the new post office was built, the log structure was deemed a historic property that was to be maintained by the municipality but not used for regular business. It was only used for school field trip blacksmithing demonstrations and open to the public for short guided tours when the town celebrated special anniversaries.

Further away from the center of town, the domiciles had been built more recently. These mostly include Cape Cods and ranchers, with the occasional tall American Foursquare jutting up above the shorter homes. There were no historic buildings in this section of town, only mid-to-late twentieth-century homes. Very few were brand new. One where a fire had destroyed the previous home. One where a dump truck had careened out of control and ran straight through the dining room of the original place, so they just knocked it all down and rebuilt it with the insurance money. Another where a wife so despised her cheating ex-husband that she ripped down the perfectly livable house where they'd once both lived and built a fresh one for herself.

The edges of the town were distinctly split. The west and north sides held only woodlands and farm properties marked by simplistic, pragmatic homes and domineering red barns with white accents. Some of the farms still had raw wood tobacco barns with open slats that let air flow through to dry the hanging tobacco leaves. Only one of them was still used for its original purpose, and in recent years it was only half-filled after harvest. The rest stored broken-down tractors and random assortments of junk.

The east and south sides of town had the most impressive residences owned by the wealthier Mancheville citizens. Almost all of the houses were in one of two communities called Towering Oaks and Mancheville Estates. Neither were gated communities, but both had the feel of one, with mostly new homes or homes that had been renovated recently enough to look brand new. Yards were large, swimming pools weren't uncommon, and luxury vehicles were in most garages.

George's home was located somewhere in between the center of the town and the edges of the municipality. If Mancheville was an archery target, the center of town would be a bullseye worth five points, while the edge of town was the outer ring worth a single point. George's home was worth three points. He'd lived in three different houses in Mancheville, all of them in the same three-point ring. He'd rarely had any kind of feeling of being stuck or forced to live in Mancheville, so it never felt odd to him that in roughly forty years, he hadn't moved outside of a couple-mile radius.

He didn't regret his decision to have lived and stayed in Mancheville. Small town, big city, and everything in-between—location doesn't have to determine your attitude. Some people simply crave negativity. Not only do they tolerate irrationality, they seek it as a way to strengthen their resolve in their own bias.

In only a month, George had created his BrainSpot pages in the same vein as what Ethan had done in his class at college. After Ethan's visit, George couldn't stop thinking about what he had shown him. Maybe, it was some kind of strange manifestation of his frustration with his friends and acquaintances. He tried very hard to be fair and balanced with Don, Alonso, and the others who butted heads. He made it a point to avoid becoming involved in arguments himself and even tried to calm others down when they did happen. He was a ready ear to listen to rants and tirades about whatever was bothering people, and he strived not to make others feel judged for their beliefs. Maybe he had grown tired of constantly being the voice of reason. Perhaps some resentment had grown from having others speak to him with the assumption that he must agree with things they were saying if he wasn't instantly defensive or combative. He could describe his new project as some kind of social experiment and that he was simply the innocent amateur social scientist looking for knowledge. If he was truthful, it also gave him a tiny little rush to feel omnipotent.

To start, George had explored BrainSpot to find two names that he could use for his pages. He had to make sure that there wasn't any person or company already using the name. He certainly didn't want his silly little project to attract some kind of ridiculous legal problem. That kind of headache wasn't worth the amusement. He settled on the names *U.S.A. Conservative Life* and *Progressive Effort*. He thought each captured what he was going for in a conservative page and a liberal page, respectively. Both names could be used on BrainSpot and didn't seem to be domains used on the web. Neither was the name of an organization, political funding group, or non-profit.

With Ethan's help through emails and a couple of phone calls, he'd grown the conservative page to nearly 2,300 followers and the liberal page to about 1,100. He'd faithfully posted at least once every day of the previous month on both pages. Ethan advised him, at least at first, to mostly use memes on his pages. People can quickly scan memes, which means they're more likely to be approved, commented on, and shared. He sometimes created his own but often used existing images on other websites and BrainSpot pages. He threw in the occasional article or video to mix things up.

Ethan showed him how to adjust certain settings and preferences to increase the chance that his posts would be visible when users scrolled through their BrainSpot feed. George trolled through other political and news pages and sent invites to active participants to join *U.S.A. Conservative Life* or *Progressive Effort*. He was pretty attentive when sending invites, being careful to send them from the page that correlated to a person's biases and leanings. Now and then, he mistakenly sent an invite for the liberal page to a conservative person or vice versa. It wasn't efficient and didn't help him grow his page following, but he did find great amusement in users' angry responses when he sent the wrong invite. Merely rejecting the invite wasn't enough for some. Often peppered with profanity and angry emojis, the most disgusted users included a personal message to hammer their rejection home.

George wanted to make sure to send page invites to his fellow bar regulars. Don took only one day to accept the opportunity to be an official follower of *U.S.A. Conservative Life* on BrainSpot. Alonso followed *Progressive Effort* almost immediately, presumably because he already had his phone in his hand when he received notification for the invite to the page. Both of them had even approved and shared a few posts from the pages in the month that they'd existed.

CHAPTER FOURTEEN

Anybody who has spent a decent amount of time in bars is familiar with the sound, but it's still jarring every time. The Mancheville Pub was slow, so the bartender took the opportunity to empty the waste can of glass bottles into the larger recycling bin just off the small kitchen. She'd kicked a doorstop with her foot until it caught underneath the door, leaving it open, so the crashing and smashing glass could be heard throughout the bar. In fact, with no other noise, it was downright startling.

Only three customers were seated at the bar: Mo, Erin, and Samuel. Not surprisingly, Samuel and the couple sat at opposite ends of the bar. He'd given a halfhearted nod in their direction when they entered, feeling obligated to at least acknowledge their presence. That was as far as their interaction had gone. It was apparent they were uncomfortable being alone with each other, but neither party felt like leaving. So, they sat in awkwardness, each of them smiling gently at the bartender when she refilled their drinks, then returning to blankness once she was gone. Mo and Erin didn't converse, choosing to instead scroll on their phones.

Samuel eventually pulled out his phone and did his own scrolling. It was true he wasn't very well-versed in technology, and he couldn't do much on his own online without becoming frustrated, but he was capable of scrolling through his BrainSpot feed. He frequently downplayed his participation in social media, writing it off as bullshit for millennials and women. He either couldn't admit it or didn't realize it, but he was pretty active on BrainSpot. It was concentrated to mostly the same conservative-style pages that Don followed. Nearly everything he now consumed could be traced back to some kind of interaction with Don on BrainSpot. He knew it wasn't much, but it felt good to follow pages and be a member of groups that supported his values—and proudly expressed their disdain for anybody opposing those beliefs. Granting a few approvals and sharing content from those pages and groups gave him some comfort in a world that seemed to be brashly and rapidly imposing change in so many ways.

All three lifted their heads and put their phones down to greet Nick when he entered. He carried a sizable cardboard box that almost covered his face. With a whoosh of air, he set the box down on a chair at one of the tables and sat down in the one next to it. The box was filled with an assortment of restaurant supplies, piled almost comically high and looking like half of it was going to fall to the floor if somebody breathed on it.

Nick caught his breath and shot a quick smile to everybody before explaining, "I'm trying out a new supplier. Gonna test out a bunch of stuff and see if the quality is good enough to make sense for the pub. Their prices are great, but it's not worth it if their stuff is shit."

The bartender set a full glass of water in front of Nick, along with several napkins.

"Thank you very much; you're sweet," he said while wiping his brow with one of the napkins. "Only thing is, their delivery is ridiculous unless you have an account with them and order a certain dollar amount. It's set up so you're forced to purchase in high volume, which explains the prices." He wiped his temples and held up his index finger that wasn't clutching the napkin. He said dramatically, "But!" and paused for effect. With his finger still raised, he continued, "If you go to one of their warehouses and pick it up yourself, they only charge a small fee for preparing the order. Of course, they don't advertise that, so you only get it if you ask them. Which I did." He grinned, obviously happy at finding what felt like a loophole, albeit a minor one. Victories had been hard to come by for some time, so he was delighted to feel like he'd enjoyed one.

It felt like somebody should respond, so Erin said politely, "That's great, Nick!"

"Thanks, I need to feel like a good businessman every once in a while. Speaking of that, if the quality is good and we can switch to this supplier, we should be able to cut enough costs to get the pub in better financial shape in the next year or so. So, I drove an hour to their closest warehouse and filled up my wife's minivan with stuff. It wouldn't be feasible to always do it that way, but it works when you're just getting a trial order."

Samuel took a gulp of beer, swallowed, and said genuinely, "Hey, we always want The Mancheville Pub around, Nick. It's a damn institution in this town."

Mo and Erin temporarily dropped their usual iciness towards Samuel and nodded approvingly, making sure Nick noticed.

"I appreciate your kind words, Sam. I want it to stick around, too, so you better believe I'll do anything I can to make that happen."

The front door opened after whoever was on the other side fumbled a second with the handle. Patrick walked in and gave a friendly wave to nobody in particular.

Samuel joked, "Hey, as long as this guy keeps showing up, you'll sell plenty of liquor!"

Patrick patted his belly paunch cheerily and said simply, "If the shoe fits." He noticed Nick sitting with the box and sauntered towards the table with a curious look on his face. He shook Nick's extended hand, then turned towards the overflowing cardboard box and began gently rummaging through it.

Nick playfully smacked his hand and said, "Hey, it's not a garage sale, Pat!"

Patrick stopped digging but did pull out a plastic tube filled with cocktail picks. He pulled out one of the wooden toothpick-like sticks with blue cellophane on the end. He stuck the non-cellophane end in his mouth and posed like a statue, letting the pick jut out from the side of his mouth. One piece of the cellophane stuck out from the pick, looking like a tiny little flag in a stiff wind.

The pick altered Pat's speech, but they could hear him ask, "Who does this remind you of?"

Everyone had a similar look of confusion on their faces.

Patrick removed the pick from between his lips and stuck it behind his ear. He started towards the bar. "You young folks won't know who I'm talking about. At least, I seriously doubt it. You're far too young to have known him when he was alive. You'd only know about him if somebody closer to my age told you about him." He continued around the bar and sat on the stool beside Samuel. "Nick and Sam, I'll give you guys another hint."

Before he could do or say anymore, George walked through the front door with a calm, unassuming look. That changed when Patrick got his attention.

"Hey, George!" He removed the cocktail pick from behind his ear, stuck it in the corner of his mouth again, and asked, "Who am I?"

George didn't appear to have any more of an idea than the rest of them.

Patrick was slightly disappointed but only let it show briefly. He let the cocktail pick drop from his mouth, and it settled beside his hand on the bar. He politely summoned the bartender, who was using a manual sweeper on the rug by the rarely-used side door. Patrick ordered a whiskey for himself, a beer for George, and a whiskey sour for Nick. He scanned the bar to make sure that everybody else had a beverage that wasn't empty.

When all of the drinks had been prepared and delivered, Patrick motioned for everybody to raise their glasses. They obliged with no argument. He licked his lips and toasted passionately, "To you and me and…"

Nick, George, and Samuel both grinned and finished the toast with him. Exuberantly and in unison, all four finished with:

"MORRIS LEE!"

The four of them laughed while Mo and Erin sat with their drinks held up, still not understanding the joke. When Patrick, George, Samuel, and Nick finished laughing, everybody finally took a sip from their drink.

Mo asked, "Who or what is Morris Lee?"

George, Samuel, and Nick both looked at Patrick, knowing he enjoyed the attention and liked playing the barroom storyteller. He didn't disappoint.

"Back in the '70s, there was a gentleman named Morris Lee. He stood out in Mancheville because he was Japanese. He came to America when he was only a teenager. I don't know the whole story, but somehow, he ended up in Mancheville. He worked down at the old brick factory for a long time and got to know a lot of people because the factory employed so many. He was very well-liked around town. He was a bar and restaurant regular. He always ordered club sandwiches. He loved American-style cuisine and talked about how he didn't eat Japanese food anymore and didn't miss it one bit once he moved to America. Anyway, he would eat his club sandwiches and then always stick the little pick with the colorful stuff at the end in the corner of his mouth. That guy must have eaten club sandwiches at least five times a week because he always seemed to have one of those little wooden picks in his mouth. He was an interesting fella.

"He and a few guys would ride together to a card game in Pittsburgh every couple of months. He loved to play poker and gin but wasn't very good at either game. I knew the guys that he went to the game with, and they said he never won. And I mean, they actually could not remember a time that he won. But you would never know it. He was just happy to play and wasn't worried about losing the money. He was certainly not wealthy, but he never had a wife or kids and lived a pretty frugal life other than the card games.

"Funny thing is, he was a master billiards player. The best shot in town and it wasn't even close. But he absolutely never gambled on it. Nobody knew why, but he refused any offer. When people know you're the best, they really want to challenge you. Players who were not even close to his skill level would offer to play him straight up for big money. He never did it. Maybe he just loved it so much that betting on it would screw up the purity of it for him. I don't know; maybe he was just lousy if he had money on it and didn't want to hurt his reputation.

"Anyway, he went to one of those card games, and something crazy happened. He won. Wasn't that much money, maybe a few hundred to the good, but the other guys said he was so happy he couldn't stop talking about it. On the ride home in the early morning, they stopped at a gas station about a half-hour from Mancheville. When the guys went inside the gas station, Morris offered to pay for the fill-up with some of his winnings. Some other guys overheard him discussing his fortunate night at the card table. They watched to see which vehicle Morris and the others got into, and they followed them the whole way to Mancheville. When Morris was dropped off at his car parked near Hank's, the guys who'd followed them pulled over about a block away. When Morris's ride drove away, they closed in on him before he could start his car and leave. They robbed him of his cash, shot him twice, and left him for dead.

"If you know anything about Nixon's presidency, you probably know that it was a pretty divided time politically and socially. Vietnam was already a controversial thing, and Nixon added fuel to that fire when he extended our involvement. Nixon was a stereotypical politician, and he didn't care if he divided people, so long as it benefited him. Some might argue that purposely dividing the American people was the main strategy in his political game. Even a small town like Mancheville was feeling the effects of the overall division of the country. It's kinda like it is today, with people all wrapped up in politics and feelin' like they need to take a side on everything and have contempt for anybody not on their side. Anyway, there was already that general tension in the town between some people. When Morris Lee was murdered, it just seemed to multiply all that tension."

Patrick waited for the bartender to swap out the old ice for new and refill his glass with whiskey. When she finished, he took a sip before continuing with his story.

"Lots of suspicion after the murder. No shortage of theories. Most of it for reasons that had nothing to with the crime itself; just people using it as an excuse to express their feelings about other stuff. Plenty of folks insisted it was race-driven. Couple of white guys just full of hate for all minorities. Maybe other minorities pissed off that Morris was so friendly with white people. Others said it was about class. A few poor folks banded together to rob a working man. Or some entitled rich kids who just wanted to have some cruel fun at a blue-collar guy's expense because they lacked concern for anybody below them in status. Politics seeped into the theories. Some local war protesters pointed out that violence like Lee's murder resulted from supporting cruel, ruthless wars that lowered our value of human life. Staunch conservatives were convinced it was a small band of hippies jonesing for their next round of dope, who, despite what they said about peace and love, would stop at nothing to get the money to support their selfish, pathetic drug habits."

Patrick had been taking intermittent sips while speaking and was empty again. He pushed the glass slightly forward and was presented with a fresh whiskey minutes later.

"Strangely, it seemed nearly everybody assumed that somebody from Mancheville must have committed the crime. People had axes to grind about others in town, and the murder was the perfect opportunity to release their anger. That all changed when news broke that the police had an eyewitness who knew all three of the men involved in the murder. They were all from West Petersburg, and they were all known criminals already. They were despised for legitimate reasons, and even people that normally never agreed on anything could agree that they were scumbags. And that's what happened. Mancheville suddenly became united in honoring Morris Lee and supporting the police in convicting the three men. It burned people that someone from another town came into Mancheville and murder one of their fellow townsmen. Ya gotta remember, people were much more tribal about the areas they lived in then. Overall, people seemed to become a little softer to each other in Mancheville, and they dropped some of the bullshit arguments that seemed so important before Lee's murder. It wasn't perfect, never is, but it was something special, I'll tell ya what.

"Around that time, people started using that toast you just heard from me. It caught on, and it was still being used frequently a decade later. Eventually, most people stopped saying it, but it was a Mancheville bar tradition for probably twenty years. Unfortunately, nobody was ever convicted because of problems in the eyewitness's story. They couldn't find the right physical evidence to convict. The town held fundraisers to pay the police force to work overtime. Folks volunteered to do stuff like mow yards and do household repairs to help the policemen's family. But to no avail, they just couldn't put those guys away. Morris was a hell of a nice guy, and he deserves to be remembered, at least. So anyway, that's that."

Patrick raised his glass again and waited for the others to do the same. He had a look of pure glee while also carrying tears in the corners of his eyes, thinking about Lee. They grinned at Patrick for being such a character and out of genuine appreciation for his story. They proclaimed together slowly but emphatically:

"TO YOU, AND ME, AND MORRIS LEE!"

CHAPTER FIFTEEN

Patrick's monologue had created a pleasant atmosphere, as only he had a way of doing, and the toast participants had spent several hours in lighthearted conversation while consuming several drinks. Customers moved in and out of the bar, but the group who'd bonded over the tribute to Morris Lee stayed intact for some time. Eventually, though, Patrick bid everyone goodbye and either moved on to another bar or went home. Samuel followed shortly after him, significantly buzzed but in a placid state. On his way out, the bartender asked him if he was walking home instead of driving. He said nothing but grinned and gave her a thumbs-up before exiting. Nick had moved to his stockroom to busy himself with emptying the boxes of restaurant supplies and placing the items in the spots where they belonged. Mo and Erin both looked tired and fairly inebriated. They'd planned to wait for Alonso, who was supposed to meet them at the pub after his night class at the community college. He was two hours late and hadn't been in touch, so they'd decided to head home when they were done with the drinks that they had in front of them.

With Patrick and Samuel gone, George was alone on his side of the bar. Although some things were not clear, he did remember the time around when somebody killed Morris Lee. He wouldn't dare diminish Patrick's enthusiasm when he was enjoying telling a tale, even if he remembered it slightly different from Patrick. As the saying goes, Patrick never lets the truth get in the way of a good story. He was known to tell some whoppers but never with the intention to hurt anybody. His fibs usually made the story's hero out to be way more legendary than they were. George never really knew if Patrick's white lies were intentional or if nostalgia just made him remember things in a more positive light. It was probably the latter, as even the average person tends to idealize or even romanticize the past. Patrick was just above average at doing so.

In this case, his record of Lee's slaying was almost entirely accurate. The only edit that George would make was to Patrick's representation of Lee as unanimously popular in town, and even then, only slightly. Lee was indeed well-liked around town. Many knew him, and a vast majority of people were very fond of him. George is one of them. The only detail that Patrick left out was the trace of vitriol that some older Mancheville residents—particularly a few World War II veterans—had towards Lee. It wasn't many, but there were certainly folks who were prejudiced against him only for his ancestry. He would have been just a young child during the war and didn't even have clear wartime memories. Any distrust or animosity towards Lee was only based on entrenched resentment towards the Japanese people as a whole and not founded on personal interaction with him.

It was understandable that Patrick would leave something like that out when recounting the period to people who were not there. It was unnecessary to pile any more negativity on an already morbid killing of a decent man. Patrick preferred to get to the part where Lee was celebrated. And bless him for that, George thought. Still, it was a reminder of how swiftly narratives can be altered simply by the teller's decision.

George's thoughts were interrupted by the movement of barstools on the other side of the bar. Mo and Erin had finished their drinks, paid their tab, and were on the way out. They detoured around the bar to say goodbye to George.

"No Don tonight?"

"I could say the same for your pal Alonso. Is he out tonight? Don has a little injury that he got when we were golfing the other day. You won't get to enjoy his company for a couple of days."

George had shot a mediocre 93 while Don had had another terrible day on the links. Even worse, this time, he'd tripped over a root in the woods after trying to hit a miracle shot between two trees with a ball sitting in a dense cluster of briars. He failed and then proceeded to twist his ankle when he tripped. That was only on the seventh hole, so he was in a foul mood for more than half the round. Afterward, his ankle had swollen some, and he'd called everybody in the foursome to complain about it and let them know he'd be recovering at his home and not to expect him at the bar until it healed.

"Ha, that sucks. But I think we'll survive without his company for a little while. Alonso was supposed to meet us after class, but he never showed, called, or texted. I have no idea."

"Maybe he was just tired and went home," Erin offered.

"That's probably what happened. Unless he's visiting Don."

"Now, I know you're messing with me!"

The three of them laughed together, and when it subsided, the couple said goodbye and turned towards the door. At the same time, it popped open loudly, and Alonso entered, sweaty and dizzyingly drunk. Even drunk, he noticed Erin's purse on her shoulder and sensed they were on the way out.

"What the hell; are you guys leaving?!"

"Dude, we waited for hours! You never even let us know you were still planning to come out."

Alonso looked at the time on his phone with glassy eyes and said, "It's pretty early; I figured you guys would be out for at least another couple of hours."

Erin, annoyed, answered sharply, "It's almost eleven o'clock, Alonso. It's not that early. We both worked today, and we have to work tomorrow."

Mo added, "Maybe if you had let us know what your plans were, we would have planned to stick around a little longer."

"Or you could have just come two hours ago when you told us you were," Erin spit out.

"Whatever, it's fine." Alonso didn't seem all that fine. "Sorry, I went back to my classmate's house after class was over tonight. He said he was gonna hang out with some friends and invited me over. They had a bunch of vodka for the weekend and were getting started on it early. Mixing up drinks and shit. I lost track of time. I shoulda texted you."

"Forget it, man, but we are heading out. Just be safe, bro."

Mo and Alonso each stuck out an arm and let their hands clap together with a loud crack. During their salutation, Erin came back to George and whispered, "Hey, please try to look after him and make sure he's okay and gets home safely."

"No problem," George whispered back.

Alonso started walking clumsily towards the rear of the pub and announced, "I'm gonna take a piss. Later, guys."

Alonso returned a few minutes later and sat beside George. They sat in silence, pretending to watch the program playing on the television above the bar. There was no sound, and the closed captioning was terrible, so it was unlikely either one could even follow what was happening on the screen.

When the bartender returned, George asked for another beer. She eyed Alonso warily while pouring George's beer and said, "I'll serve you, Alonso, but you gotta keep it under control. If you start tripping over stools, or arguing, or getting loud, then you're done."

Alonso held up both arms to show his submission to her rule. "No worries. I'll just have whatever George is having." He already seemed a bit soberer than when he'd arrived, but it was obvious that he wasn't well. Alonso pretty much operated in a constant agitation state, but he seemed even more distressed than usual. George pointed at the beer that the bartender had cautiously served Alonso.

"You sure that's a good idea?"

"He's gonna O.D., I just know it. I just don't see how he won't." Alonso squeezed his temples.

"Who?"

"I'm just such a goddamn mess myself, and I'm supposed to help him get straight. I mean, I at least don't do drugs, but I'm not exactly the most together person. I drink too much, I don't even know if going to college is going to work out, and I get so depressed over bad shit that happens in our country."

"Who are you talking about?"

Alonso still didn't face George, but he finally answered, "My brother."

"I don't think I've ever met him. What kind of problem has he got?"

"Heroin. Like so many damn people. Same kind of story as a million others. He hurt himself playing soccer in high school, and they prescribed him pain shit. I think he was messing around with other stuff anyway, but he wasn't an addict. He used his prescription and maxed out the refills. Started taking Oxies that he got from a friend of a friend from Philly. Heroin dealers around here were quick to help him out and give him a cheaper option. He lives with his girlfriend in a room above a bar a couple of towns over in Tobosburg. He might have kicked the shit if he hadn't moved in with her. She's pretty much a junkie too, but she strips at a club and makes enough money to keep their room." Alonso seemed like he wanted to say more but ran out of energy to do so. He was on the verge of tears.

"I'm very sorry to hear that, Alonso. I've seen plenty of drunks and addicts in my day, but this epidemic is something like I've never seen before. Is he older or younger?"

"He's older by five years."

"It's easy for an older sibling to feel horrible about their mistakes and believe that they're largely responsible for any wrong choices that their younger siblings make. The guilt over feeling like a failure as a role model can be burdensome. Of course, we all have to make our way in life. I'm sure that, despite some anger or frustration you might have with your brother, you don't hold him responsible."

"No, I don't. I hate that his life is a wreck, but I don't blame him for my shit."

"There isn't a lot to say to someone, specifically about their addiction, when they're buried in it. At least nothing that hasn't probably been repeated time and time. It's not based on logical thinking. The only thing that I'd suggest is to use his clearheaded moments to let him know that he doesn't need to add anything extra to his struggle regarding you. Doesn't mean letting him off the hook for his behavior. But if he hears that, it might be the thing he needs to survive a little bit longer and find a way out."

A tear finally did fall down Alonso's cheek, and he quickly swiped it away with a cocktail napkin. He nodded but said nothing back to George.

They sat for another hour, only throwing in casual remarks about the show on the television that still didn't have any sound. It was a rerun of a popular sitcom, so both probably saw it before. With that prior knowledge, piecing together some of the closed captioning and a little bit of physical humor, they laughed a few times.

Eventually, George let Alonso know that he was going to head home. He said mildly, "I promised Erin that I would make sure you get home safely."

"I know I shouldn't have driven here, but I'll leave my car. Don't worry, George; I scheduled an Uber to pick me up and get me home. I promise I'm good." He held up his phone as if to prove he had a ride. It was quick, and George didn't see any details about the ride on the screen, but he trusted that Alonso wouldn't lie in this instance. He paid his tab and exited, giving Alonso a light pat on the shoulder along the way.

CHAPTER SIXTEEN

While George had trusted Alonso when he told him he'd arranged a ride, there was still a flying gnat of concern buzzing around George's head in the morning. Alonso could be a bit of a wild card, so it wouldn't surprise George if Alonso had scheduled the ride and then canceled it after George left. Not to purposely lie to George, but simply because he was prone to giving in to his impulses. When booking the ride, it was highly likely he had full intention to follow through on it. That could change on a whim. Somebody would show up, and Alonso would convince himself that he needed to have a drink with the person, sure that George would understand his obligation to do so. He might get a text message that pissed him off, and he'd immediately order a beer to calm himself down, certain that George would have sympathy for him and understand his need to relax. Or Alonso might just decide that getting an Uber was too expensive or annoying.

George was relieved when he logged on to BrainSpot and saw that Alonso had been active recently. The timestamps on multiple comments he made were less than twenty minutes old. Most likely, that meant that he'd simply taken the Uber home and kept himself out of any trouble. George hoped that was true. He was annoyed with himself that he'd left before knowing for sure that Alonso had called it a night and left safely for home. He didn't take it lightly when somebody pointed out that a person might need somebody to look after them at the bar. George knew way too many dreadful things that had happened to people who didn't have somebody to protect them when they lost control. It was silly that he didn't just wait it out after promising Erin that he'd watch Alonso.

If he was still writing in his blog, he might have written a post about it just as a means of catharsis. Explore his thoughts a little bit and eventually realize that he shouldn't feel too guilty about another adult—even if Alonso barely qualified—drinking far too much and putting himself in dangerous situations. That it's nice to be concerned, but a grown man has to be accountable for himself.

As it was, he had indefinitely abandoned his blog. Not surprisingly, there wasn't an uprising from his fans, begging for him to continue posting. He'd been spending nearly all of his time in front of his computer monitor working on the *U.S.A. Conservative Life* and *Progressive Effort* BrainSpot pages that he'd created. He still had no endgame to his project, no grand purpose beyond his amusement, yet his pages were growing slowly but surely. He was by no means building an empire, but he gained roughly a dozen followers each day. Ethan even remarked that the pages might get to a point where he could set up paid ads and receive ad revenue when people clicked on them. Ethan pointed out that it would be very little money, but it might still be worth the effort to set them up in BrainSpot in a couple of months. George would get a kick out of that if it ever happened. He planned to buy a new putter if the passive income stream ever became a reality.

Until this point, he'd only posted items on the pages that were obviously biased but not necessarily incendiary. He even threw in the occasional news story that just had boring facts, so the page didn't seem too over-the-top. That was a suggestion from Ethan. He said that the more benign news stories lend some credibility to the pages, which helps avoid targeting from BrainSpot for account bans or suspensions because of complaints and reporting from people who oppose the page. George searched news sites to specifically find articles and videos that nobody was arguing about, clicking through page after page to find content with barren comment threads that proved readers and viewers either didn't care about the topic or were in general agreement about it. This was often harder than expected.

Yet, he had the urge to crank his pages up a notch and see if he could share some things that would cause a stir. Even if it was just a few posts, he wanted to get a little dicey just to see what happened. It was so against his normal behavior to do anything just to get a rise out of people. He rarely even made sarcastic jokes or teased people, on the off chance that it might offend them. It was less of a matter of altruism than some thought. George very much cared for others, but he also felt deep anxiety if he thought somebody had misinterpreted something he said. Staying on the safer side in most conversations was as much a tactic to avoid feeling uneasy as it was to prevent others' discomfort. That's what made the possibility of purposely provoking people on his pages appealing–the lack of that awkwardness present if he did it in person.

He perused various political news outlets for hours, scanning headlines and reading articles to find bizarre and ridiculous stories. Whenever he found something crazy, he searched more to see if it was true or not. His goal was to find either a completely contrived or wildly taken-out-of-context piece from both sides of the political spectrum. He planned to post them simultaneously and see if they got any response, a bit of an experiment to see if people would let their bias overcome their common sense and accept the story as true. In all honesty, despite seeing a lot of absurd behavior on the web, George didn't expect many reactions. Maybe a person or two would react without thinking it through first. But surely someone from each page would immediately point out that the stories were bogus. Eventually, he found a piece for each page that satisfied him.

The article he chose for *U.S.A. Conservative Life* had the headline: **NYC mayor approves legislation requiring one mosque for every Christian church.**

The article's premise was that the mayor of New York City had created a law that required there to be a house of worship for every religion within planned sections throughout the city. Each area was approximately five square miles, depending on the physical layout. If there was not a house of worship for a recognized religion within a section, the city government would allow zoning to build one or designate an existing space to that religion. The government would only enforce the rule if a citizen or group made a formal request to the city to create the house of worship. If necessary, the government would employ eminent domain to seize buildings or land. The article spun the idea to make it seem like the government was making a concerted effort to build mosques to weaken Christian influence on the city.

Of course, the article wasn't just misrepresenting the law—it was creating it out of thin air. The mayor only said he envisioned a city that, among other things, boasted blocks with all kinds of places to worship, with every religion respected so long as it was peaceful and benefited the community. It was just a minor tidbit from a speech intended to gain support from various constituents. The mayor made no law, regulation, or even suggestion to establish new houses of worship with force.

The article George chose for *Progressive Effort* had the headline: **Republican VP: Allowing rape victim abortions may lead women to try to get raped.**

The gist of the piece was that the current Republican Vice President, while stumping in the Midwest to win the election, had made some incredibly inflammatory arguments about rape and abortions. He reportedly said that women should not abort even in instances of rape. The vice president continued by saying that one of the reasons rape victim abortions should not occur is that it may lead women to try to get raped to take advantage of the procedure to get several days off from work. The article creator even went so far as to create a silent video with subtitles that put these words in his mouth.

Despite having a track record of tone-deaf remarks about various female health issues and sexual issues, the vice president had never even come close to saying something so crass. The vice president had even successfully sued the creators of the story. Most media outlets swiftly pulled the original content, but online social media users had created hundreds of reproductions and recreations of the story. Anyone could still easily find versions of the story deeming the information to be factual.

There may have been a moment of hesitation before posting, but not much. George felt a dash of peculiar excitement despite not wanting to support false narratives. Ethically, it was not his normal conduct. He'd never been one to spread even the most trivial rumors. He'd even reacted somewhat harshly in the past on the rare occasions that Anna shared local gossip before doing her due diligence to determine its veracity. Now he was doing it himself on a more extensive and potentially more damaging scale. But George was fixated on finding out the response to the fraudulent articles that he shared.

After working on his BrainSpot pages, he'd remembered that he needed to pick up his cholesterol medication at the pharmacy.

George put his Explorer into reverse and backed out of the driveway. The SUV was ten years old, but George had owned it since it was new and had always maintained it carefully. He had minimal mechanical aptitude himself, but he had a mechanic he trusted and allowed him to do whatever preventative maintenance or recommended repairs. He rarely felt any shudders, squeaks, slips, or whines from the vehicle, and only when it was well below freezing outside.

That certainly wasn't a current problem in Mancheville. George cranked the knob for the fan the whole way to maximum power, enjoying the tactile little clicks as he surpassed each power level. When he felt resistance, he released any pressure and felt the knob slip into the last spot. After driving a few blocks on the quiet street, the air conditioning finally reached a cold state, and he closed his eyes for one or two seconds to enjoy the air blasting his cheek and left forearm.

It was only a short drive to the pharmacy, and he enjoyed the music on the radio, so he felt like he arrived in no time. One of those quick trips across town, where you get to your destination and have almost no recollection of the drive you made. When it's a bit scary, the realization that you just operated a machine that weighs over a ton without using a single conscious, attentive thought to do so. He sat inside the truck with the air conditioning still whooshing and let the last song play out before shutting off the engine and stepping out of the vehicle.

George walked across the nearly empty parking, carefully avoiding the repaired cracks where the tar was turning to a sticky adhesive in the sun. If you step in an especially goopy one, it can be a real pain in the ass. The tar made him think of pine tar, which reminded him of baseball and the Phillies. They'd completed a home series against the Brewers two nights ago, and they were in Toronto to play the Blue Jays tonight, he remembered. The Blue Jays conjured up the memory of the Phillies losing to them in the World Series in 1993. He silently cursed Joe Carter for hitting the championship-clinching home run. George and Anna went to a friend's home to watch the game. They were a married couple that Anna had chatted up at a junior high music concert. Both couples were there to see their daughters perform, and both daughters happened to play the flute, which was something of an icebreaker to move the conversation beyond just pleasantries. For Anna, that is. George always made it a point to be very courteous to strangers, but he rarely engaged in a lengthy exchange with somebody he didn't know. Anna was better at that, and that's how they ended up at the Gringels' house to watch Joe Carter break Philadelphia's heart.

He had not been pleasant after the loss—nothing major but cranky enough to embarrass Anna, and they left the Gringels' place very shortly after the game. He didn't think he'd acted like too much of a jerk, but he had to admit it probably set the tone for his relationship with them. Anna became decent friends with the wife, but George never moved beyond acquaintance level with either of them. After Anna had passed, they were at the funeral, but he hadn't spoken with them since. The same thing happened with a few other couples, too. George and Anna had always kept a relatively small circle of friends, but it diminished even more after her passing. It wasn't that he made an effort to avoid people; he'd simply never been the one to initiate get-togethers and parties and other social gatherings. When you aren't involved in things like that, it's easy to lose touch. As a result, his golf foursome and the regulars at The Mancheville Pub, The Night's Quest, and Hank's became his primary social group.

When he got to the automatic door, he stood to the side so the sensor wouldn't detect his body. He checked each sneaker, making sure he'd avoided the parking lot tar. He didn't want to track it in the store and gunk up the vacuum for whoever had to clean when the store closed. Satisfied that he was tar-free, he stood in front of the doors until they opened with a delicate snapping sound. He entered and let out an audible satisfied exhale when he felt the initial burst of cool air on his shoulders and scalp.

Past the makeup, toys, and candles, around the cold medication and bottles of pain pills, and through the aisle of athletic tape and bandages, he finally came to the pharmacy counter. There were two customers in line: one senior citizen woman in front and a middle-aged woman standing behind her, scrolling on her phone. On either side of the counter, there were small benches. George sat down on the empty one. The other one held a young man either in his late teens or early twenties. He had his eyes fixed on the ceiling, so George was able to gaze at him for a moment.

He felt bad thinking it but couldn't help noticing that the young guy looked dreadful. It seemed like he was in his mid-twenties, but you had to examine him for a few minutes to realize it. His hair wasn't overly long, but it stuck out in all directions. His eyes were so hollow and dark that somebody could mistake them for a pair of black eyes at a glance. He had a week or more of raw, untrimmed scruff. His too-long blue jeans had asymmetrical fringes on each pant leg, with chunks of material clumped and crusted together in places. His hooded sweatshirt was massive, and the size of it shrouded his body enough that it was hard to tell if he was skinny, fat, or somewhere in between.

Anybody in that outfit must be sick and experiencing some strange body temperature issues, thought George. Alonso's comments about his brother quickly came to George's mind. Was the young man sick because he was desperately in need of filling his Oxy prescription? Was his prescription even legitimate? Was he just sitting there listening to people fill their prescriptions, waiting for the next person to receive a bottle of pain pills so that he could rob them in the parking lot?

Maybe it was Alonso's brother. The age would be about right. From what Alonso said, he was already pretty deep into heroin, but he certainly wouldn't turn down a fresh bottle of Oxies if he could get his hands on them. Maybe it was a freak coincidence that he happened to be present at the pharmacy when George was there for his cholesterol pill pickup.

He stopped himself from thinking any further about it; his thoughts were getting away from him. There was still a chance that the young fellow just looked like shit because he was genuinely sick from some kind of virus or bug. Perhaps he didn't have anybody to drive him to the pharmacy, so he had to make the trip himself. He might just be suffering through absolutely no fault of his own, just a random pummeling of his immune system not caused by indulging in narcotics. Either way, George felt sorry for the miserable guy.

"Next."

The pharmacist's signaling for the next person in line knocked George back to reality and out of his ponderings. He realized that both women had gone through the line, and it was only now he and the young man. George looked over at him, pointing towards the counter as if to say, 'go ahead.'

He croaked out, "I have to wait for mine to be filled; it isn't ready yet. It's your turn." It sounded quite painful, and he didn't seem like he wanted to struggle through any more words.

"Okay, thanks," George answered with a gentle nod in his direction.

They'd already prepared his medicine, so his transaction was quick, and he was back in his Explorer in very little time. He experienced another trip where his subconscious took over the driving, and he had no clear memory of how he got to his destination. George never even turned on the radio. There was no music or phone call or any other outside distraction. The entire ride, he'd thought about the disheveled twenty-something at the pharmacy. He thought about Alonso and his brother. He thought about people in his past who'd were addicted to alcohol and drugs. He thought about the bars he frequented and what they represented in his life, and the lives of those he spent time with regularly. And then he was home.

After arriving, Patrick called to invite him over to take a dip in his pool and have some drinks on the deck. Having nothing better to do the rest of the day, he'd agreed to meet in an hour or so. In the meantime, he thought he'd jump on BrainSpot to see if anything interesting was happening on his pages. It hadn't been long since posting, so he had little expectation of activity beyond possibly one or two approvals or maybe a share.

Both posts had gone viral—at least as far as George was concerned—garnering more attention than anything he'd had on his pages. The post on *U.S.A. Conservative Life* had 238 approvals, 69 shares, and 48 comments, while the one on *Progressive Effort* had slightly less of both at 196 approvals, 15 shares, and 24 comments.

George was excited at the response he'd gotten from his posts. Growing his pages had been a slow, steady crawl. It was exhilarating to see the numbers that had appeared under his posts in such a short period.

He was less exhilarated when he read through the comments and saw who had made most of them. The timestamps indicated that it had all started after Don left a comment on the most recent post on *U.S.A. Conservative Life*. A snarky response from Alonso came after that. They went back and forth on that thread, nasty comment for nasty comment. Alonso commented on the *Progressive Effort* post. Don responded to that, and their clash spilled into that thread. There were other stray comments, some even engaging in little arguments of their own, but no other users even had a chance to chime in on Don and Alonso's comment war.

Don: *"THE OVERTAKING OF AMERICA BY MOSLEMS CONTINUES! HOW DO AMERICANS STAND FOR THIS?! O THAT'S RIGHT ITS NYC, WHICH IS BARELY AMERICA. JUST LIKE COMMIEFORNIA, TRASH CITIES FULL OF PEOPLE WHO HATE THIS COUNTRY AND EVERYTHING IT STANDS FOR"*

Alonso: *"WTF. Why do you think giving another religion that's not Christian a fair piece of the pie to be a direct threat to ur life? Other cultures can have a chance, not just yours!"*

Don: *"DON'T REALLY CARE TO HEAR YOUR OPINION, I'VE HEARD YOUR LIBERAL BS AND I DON'T CARE TO HEAR IT ANYMORE. YOUR PRACTICALLY STILL A KID, YOUR CLUELESS"*

Alonso: *"You just write me off because I'm liberal, just like every other conservative asshat. Maybe you should stop praying to go back in time to some fakeass world you thought was better"*

Don: *"AND YOU DON'T KNOW ANYTHING ABOUT IT. BECAUSE WE HAVE TO WIPE THE ASSES OF HELPLESS YOUNG FOLKS AND PAY THE BILLS OF LAZY PEOPLE WEVE LOST SO MUCH."*

Alonso: *"Get off ur high horse, you act like your tax money has personally covered every single person that ever used welfare or some kind of government program"*

Don: *"MY TAX MONEY HAS DONE PLENTY, AND I NEVER HAD TO ASK FOR A PENNY OF HELP FROM ANYBODY"*

Alonso: *"ok boomer"*

Don: *"WHAT THE HELL DOS THAT HAVE TO DO WITH ANYTHING? IS THAT ALL YOU GOT?"*

Alonso: *"Do you have any idea how much easier it was for your generation? You could pay for college by working a part-time job. It's ridiculous."*

Don: *"NO SURPRISE. YOULL VOTE FOR THE FIRST PERSON TO GUARANTEE YOU FREE COLLEGE. THE GENERATION OF HANDOUTS AND ENTITLEMENT."*

Alonso: *"Ur crazy. I should be able to go to school w/ out being insanely in debt as soon as I graduate. That's not asking for free college or any handout."*

Don: *"MAYBE PEOPLE SHOULD STOP GETTING THEIR DEGREES IN BASKET WEAVING AND ACTUALLY STUDY SOMETHING THAT THEY CAN MAKE MONEY WITH"*

Alonso: *"Literally nobody studies basket-weaving in college. Why does every dumbass boomer use that as a reference?"*

Don: *"ITS TO MAKE A POINT. MIGHT NOT BE BASKET-WEAVING. BUT ITS SOME USELESS DEGREE AND THE*

STUDENT ENDS UP WORKING AT MCDONALDS PRO-
TESTING FOR $15 AN HOUR"

Alonso: *"Maybe the job market would be better if old white rich dudes
weren't scared to hire women, or people of color, or people that might think a little
differently than them!"*

Don: *"I WONDERED HOW LONG IT WOULD TAKE FOR
THE RACE CARD TO COME OUT. GENDER BS AND WHITE
MEN BEING THE CAUSE OF EVERYBODY'S PROBLEMS.
SO TYPICAL"*

Alonso: *"Maybe if you knew how to treat women right, your wife wouldn't
have left you. Good for her, she's much better off."*

Don: *"YOU HAVE TO THROW INSULTS BECAUSE YOU
HAVE NO BETTER ARGUMENT FOR THINGS. AT LEAST
SOMEBODY WAS INTERESTED IN ME AT SOME POINT.
NOBODY CARES ABOUT BETA MALES LIKE YOU!"*

That was where they stopped on the *U.S.A. Conservative Life*
thread. Their interaction on the *Progressive Life* thread was much
shorter but no less nasty.

Alonso: *"The vice president is a disgusting, vile scumbag with no concern
but to pander to fake Christians, so he keeps getting political positions. No matter the situation, he claims to never want abortions to happen, but he doesn't give
a shit about the babies once they're out of the womb. Using his religion as a reason
to deny women's right to choose what's best for them. Asshole."*

Don: *"HOW CAN YOU BE SO PASSIONATE ABOUT MUR-
DERING BABIES?"*

Alonso: *"It's a fetus, not a baby. How can you care so much about supporting a guy who would say such horrific things about women? Oh, that's right,
you've pretty much shown that you think women are second-class citizens."*

Don: *"YOU COULD USE A LITTLE CHRISTIANITY IN
YOUR LIFE. YOU MIGHT LEARN A LITTLE BIT ABOUT
DISCIPLINE AND RESPONSIBILITY. MAYBE YOU HAVE A
CHANCE TO CHANGE, UNLIKE YOUR JUNKIE BROTHER"*

Alonso: *"Screw you, you don't know anything about my brother!"*

Don: *"YOU DON'T KNOW ANYTHING ABOUT MY MAR-
RIAGE, BUT IT DIDN'T STOP YOU FROM GETTING
PERSONAL"*

Alonso: *"Who are you to talk about my bother? How many decades have
you spent sitting at a bar slamming drinks and doing nothing with your life?"*

Don: *"ARE YOU WORRIED YOUR BROTHER AND HIS TRASH GIRLFRIEND MIGHT GET TO HIGH ONE NIGHT AND ACCIDENTALLY GET HER PREGNANT? IS THAT WHY YOURE SO WORRIED ABOUT THEM HAVING THE RIGHT TO KILL A UNBORN BABY?"*

There was no response from Alonso.

George was a bit scared and ashamed about all of it. He had the ability to pull the content instantly, but despite his discomfort, he didn't. He had certainly not set out to purposely cause Don and Alonso to engage in such brutal digital battle with each other, but now it was raging.

Still, he let the posts remain live on his pages, curious to see where it all might lead. He had to see just how high all of those numbers could reach. Maybe it was a pent-up annoyance from years of writing a blog that he knew nobody read. Perhaps he was just a bored old man with little else to be passionate about anymore. He didn't know exactly why. The posts remained available to the world, or at least the little worlds he'd helped create through his pages.

CHAPTER SEVENTEEN

Patrick wasn't from the most affluent section of town, somewhere in the median range, but he did have a pool. He and Charlene lived in a modest but well-kempt Colonial not far from where George lived. It had bleach-white siding and black shutters, and the only remotely flashy thing about the home was the candy apple red front door. For reasons even Charlene wasn't sure of, Patrick insisted on always having a snazzy red door, and he maintained a fresh coat of glossy paint on it that was never more than a year old.

The pool was a simple aboveground type, but it was plenty satisfactory for cooling George down when it was blazing hot. He wasn't much of a swimmer, but he did occasionally take advantage of Patrick and Charlene's open invitation to take a dip any time he wanted. They had a nice little setup, a sizable deck adjoining the pool, and a small pavilion where they hosted family and friends, and Patrick played master of the grill while getting drunk on cold gin and lemonades.

"Georgeyboy!"

He heard Patrick before he saw him. The friendly greeting came from the shadows of the pavilion, where it was already dark, and a gray haze of smoke hovered, further veiling the area where Patrick was presumably standing. The floating rings and lounger in the pool were still moving around, and there was little wind, so Patrick had recently gotten out and was probably checking on whatever he had cooking on the grill.

He stepped outside of the pavilion with a drink in one hand and a sizable spatula in the other, clad only in faded blue swim trunks and sandals. Oversized sunglasses seemed to cover over half of his face. George recognized them as the same style that Patrick had been wearing since the late '70s. Because both hands were full, Patrick stuck out his fist that held the spatula to give George a fist bump in place of a handshake.

"What's on the grill today?"

"Just a couple burgers and sausages, nothing special really. Charlene cleaned out the freezer, and these were old enough that she said we should just get rid of them rather than sticking them back in. Figured I might as well just grill 'em up rather than toss 'em."

"Sounds good to me. I wouldn't mind helping get rid of some."

"That's what I figured, so I gave you a call. What's your pleasure, my good man?"

"I'll take one of each if that works."

"Sure does. Charlene will be out shortly with some buns, condiments, and potato chips. Want a drink?"

"I do. What are my options?"

"Oh, you know we always have a wide variety. Just about any liquor you could ask for. The kegerator has lager and a stout right now."

George was pretty sure what the answer was, but he asked anyway, "What're you drinking there?"

"My poolside standby, of course, gin and some lem-o-nade." Just as reliable as his poolside drink choice was his love of pronouncing it with a long, exaggerated 'o' in the middle of the word 'lemonade.' He laid down the spatula and used two fingers to pick up a half-smoked cigarette from an ashtray that sat on a wide log acting as an end table beside the grill. He took a brief drag from it and then put it out.

"I'll have the same; sounds like a pretty great choice for a hot day."

"You sure? You can have whatever you like."

"Yep, I'm sure."

Patrick nodded and opened up the mini-fridge, pulling out a nearly full pitcher of lemonade.

"I'm surprised you're only that far into the lemonade. Haven't been out long?"

"It's the second pitcher of the day," Patrick answered with a grin, "I've got a couple hours on you." He grabbed a highball glass that was sitting upside down on a tray on top of the mini-fridge. A lunchbox-sized cooler sat beside the tray. He pushed a button while flipping the lid back in one motion and then scooped out some of the ice inside with the glass. He smacked the lid shut with his free hand and set the highball glass on the picnic table. He pulled out a half-filled, bright blue bottle of gin from the fridge and started slowly pouring.

"When"

Patrick looked at George with a smile and let just the tiniest amount more gin fall into the glass before filling it the rest of the way with lemonade. He pulled a straw from a box sitting on the tray beside two other glasses. He gave the drink a brief stir before letting the straw drop and handed it to George.

"How goes it, George?"

George instantly thought of his posts on BrainSpot and the trouble they were causing—or at least helping to cause—between Don and Alonso. Patrick might be a good person to talk with about the situation. His knowledge of the internet was minimal, but he was a good one to speak to when you needed an ear with a nonjudgmental person attached. With his gift of gab, Patrick was willing to discuss nearly anything. George didn't feel like discussing it just yet, though, so he packed it away for consideration after a couple of gin and lemonades.

"Pretty much the norm, I guess," said George, burying his worries for at least the time being.

"Same. We finalized our plans for that cruise we're taking in September. Charlene's excited. Frankly, I'm probably just as happy drinking by the pool, but I'm sure we'll have a good time. She's already making a list of the new clothes we need to buy for the trip. I don't know why I need new shit, but she likes it. Part of the fun of the whole thing, I suppose."

"I think she might be right if new trunks are on the list," said George with a gesture towards Patrick's faded pair.

Patrick laughed and relented, "I guess I can't argue with that."

As if she'd heard her name spoken, Charlene came out the back door with a grocery bag containing buns and potato chips. She held both a bottle of ketchup and mustard by the neck in her other hand. She wore a wide brim hat and a cover-up over what appeared to be a floral two-piece, although it was difficult to tell for sure. The cover-up material was flowy and light but still dense enough to mostly hide what was underneath.

"Regular chips okay? We might have barbeque in the pantry, but I'm not sure."

"Regular will work for me," George answered with an appreciative smile.

"I think there's American cheese in the fridge out here. We have lettuce and tomatoes inside, but I didn't cut them up yet. No onions, though. Would you like me to bring those out?"

"No, don't trouble yourself. Just ketchup and mustard will do for me."

Patrick held up a finger. "That reminds me, would you like cheese on your burger, George?"

"Yes, please."

"I'll toss the cheese on now; they're almost done. Charlene, cheese?"

"I'm just having a sausage. Thanks, though."

"You got it."

After they all ate, Patrick and Charlene laid out on chaise loungers while George got in the pool to cool off. He set his drink on the ledge of the pool and submerged himself into the crystal water. Surfacing, he gently sprayed out water from both corners of his mouth and rubbed his eyes to restore his vision. George grabbed a floating ring and rested his arms on the vinyl that was warm from the sun, slowly pushing himself towards his drink to grab it from the ledge. He glided around the pool, occasionally using his free hand to splash water on his face and shoulders, which only worked for a few minutes. He'd used the powder room just inside the house after eating and applied some spray sunscreen that was sitting out on the corner. He hoped it was enough to—at the very least—keep the burn to a minimum.

George floated around the pool for about half an hour. He had several spans where he was relaxed for a few minutes, letting his eyelids fall so he could go into a sort of meditation just short of sleep. But he spent a majority of his floating time staring into the air or gazing into the water, ruminating on the BrainSpot posts.

"Oh, damn. I was supposed to call Karen about going to the vineyard next weekend. I have to go call her." Charlene rose from her lounger and stuck her wide brim on before flip-flopping down the deck stairs and striding inside.

Patrick rose, straddling the lounger while finishing his latest drink. Once it was empty, he reached down towards George for his glass. He carefully tip-toed off the deck in his bare feet, so no stray wood slivers poked into the bottom of his feet, returning moments later with two fresh drinks and handed one to George.

"Thanks." George considered bringing up his concerns to Patrick. Before he could, Patrick spoke first.

"You seem a little preoccupied, George. Something wrong?"

"As a matter of fact, I am preoccupied. I'm just not sure I can explain it properly, so you'll understand. It's kind of an awkward situation."

"Well, you're welcome to try. Couldn't hurt." Patrick sat on the lounger and swung his legs to the side while stretching his back from side to side. He sat his glass on the little table between the two loungers without taking a sip, as if to signify he was genuinely listening.

George tried his best to explain to Patrick what was going on, although it was somewhat tough to convey it to somebody who didn't participate in social media. Patrick seemed to grasp the circumstances well enough.

"I'm sure there are things I don't completely understand, but there's no question that I've seen it change how some people interact with each other. Don gets so hopping mad he can barely be contained some nights. I guess it's easier to say it when you're looking from the outside in, but it just seems like people are getting worked up over a whole lotta nothing. Obviously, it doesn't feel like nothin' to them. People have always argued in bars, and you and I can personally attest that they have in Mancheville. But it's different when their anger starts over something on the computer at home, and they come into the bar ready to argue. I hate to see it, George, I really do. It's a damn shame."

"I know, and now I feel like I'm causing it. It was just something to entertain myself. I'm not forcing them to comment on the posts and get pissed off at each other. I invited people I know to the pages. I expected that I might see Don or Alonso comment on something, maybe even get into tiffs with strangers, but I never really considered that something ugly would arise between them on my pages. They are well aware of each other's BrainSpot activity, even going so far as to post things that are passive-aggressive to each other. But I've never seen them engage in a full-blown argument on the internet. It's not good at all, because they say things behind their computer that they would never say across the bar. They get heated at Hank's, but there are still boundaries that they don't cross."

"You should be concerned, but you're right in that they're still accountable for their own behavior. Doesn't seem like there's much reward for you, though. I'd want to end my part in all of that if I were you."

George only answered with a subtle, contemplative nod.

Charlene came out of the house in the same garb. She seemed content, so she must have been able to get in touch with Karen to make their plans for next weekend. She carried a yellow towel against her chest with one hand and a paperback in the other. It was good there was no wind; just the rush of air from her walking pace pushed the brim of her hat upwards at an awkward angle. Any whoosh of breeze would have sent it flying.

"I brought you a towel, George," she said as she came up the deck steps.

"Just in time. Thanks, Charlene." And it was perfect timing; he had just ascended the ladder to get out of the pool.

"Take the other chaise; I'm getting in."

"Great, I will." George gave himself a quick rub on his back, butt, and legs just to get the bulk of the water off himself. The sun would make short work of anything else.

She plucked off her hat and removed her cover-up, hanging it neatly over the railing of the deck. She did indeed have on a two-piece decorated with a pattern of tiny flowers. It was impressive that she had the confidence to wear a two-piece, but not surprising with her body. She had some wrinkle rings near her armpits and her skin bunched up in strange ways at her joints and on her shoulder blades, but that was the only evidence that she was in her late sixties. She had a wonderfully even tan with symmetrically placed runs of small freckles on the sides of her thighs like the speckles on the body of a brown trout. Her behind was still taught, with only one precise crease at the base of each cheek. Her breasts were not large but hung heavily. Not sagging, just a natural dangle that still allowed them to retain a youthful orb shape.

George felt something unusual; Charlene's body was turning him on. He hadn't been sexual at all since Anne had passed, and he only just realized it. His member wasn't even close to erect, but George recognized the familiar rush of blood to his midsection that hadn't occurred in ages. He enjoyed it for a moment and watched her in his periphery without staring. She went into the water until it reached halfway up her calves and then jumped in with her fingers squeezing her nose like a child. Patrick was faced the other way, watching their neighbor tend to their dog in the yard. George cursed himself for forgetting his sunglasses, as that would have made his quick gazing session easier.

And just like that, it was gone. George felt a rush of foolishness for gawking at his friend's wife. He thought nothing of it when he was younger. Plenty of his friends had attractive wives and girlfriends, and he'd never considered it any kind of morally questionable thing to notice that and appreciate it. Cheating on Anne was never a consideration, nor was fooling around with a friend's significant other. And he still didn't have intentions of doing the latter.

But now, he felt stupid. Like a dirty old man, even though Charlene was almost the same age as him. Hell, he didn't even know if he could perform sexually without going to the doctor and getting a prescription to give him some kind of unnatural, contrived hard-on. He immediately changed his gaze to watch the neighbor that had Patrick's attention. It seemed like anything that gave him a rush of youthful energy these days ultimately just turned into a stark reminder of his old age. It would almost be better if he didn't have those bursts because the comedown was brutal. Maybe it was time to stop with the little brain exercises to try to stay sharp. Should he just interact with Ethan more like a grandfather instead of a buddy? Perhaps he should finally cut the bars out of his life. Was he just going in some pathetic attempt to feel like he was part of the action and excitement?

"Sorry to run, but I just realized I have to grab a prescription at the pharmacy." He had, of course, already picked it up, but it was the first thing he could think of as an excuse to leave without it seeming strange. Both Patrick and Charlene bid goodbye to him. Charlene asked if he was sure he had to go and said he was welcome to stay as long as he wanted. She was being genuinely nice, and neither of them seemed concerned or insulted about him leaving somewhat abruptly.

He didn't know the answers to the questions he was asking himself but wanted to escape the discomfort he was feeling from his arousal over Charlene's presence. George made his way around the house with more thoughts running through his head. Was that what this BrainSpot nonsense was all about, forcefully trying to be part of something just to feel some dazzle of youth?

When he arrived home, the scene on BrainSpot did nothing to calm his anxieties. Samuel had jumped to Don's defense, and he was also now shooting comment insults to Alonso, which had prompted Mo and Erin to jump in on Alonso's side. There were even other people from Mancheville throwing in jabs and talking points. George felt a queasiness growing in his stomach as he read through the threads.

George found the area on his BrainSpot dashboard to turn the pages private so nobody could view them anymore. He clicked where he needed to click, selected the settings that Ethan had shown him, and then clicked the final button to apply the changes. He logged out of his account and then tried to view his pages like a stranger. They came up as unavailable, and George was satisfied that he'd correctly made the changes. He shut down his computer and moved to the couch to try his best to take a nap.

CHAPTER EIGHTEEN

"Are ya tired of hearing it yet, folks? Hopefully, you're not at your breaking point because this heatwave sure isn't!"

The weatherman had a steady grin on his face despite delivering bad news for just about everybody but air conditioner repair businesses. As is often the case, the meteorologist was in the classic 'don't shoot the messenger' situation. It's no secret that many people get pissed off at the weatherman when they hear a report that doesn't please them. Perhaps if the weather folks didn't always maintain a giant grin when reporting the weather, people might like them better.

"We're looking at the hottest temperatures we've seen all summer—believe it or not! A true scorcher out there with little wind to help out the situation. We'll be seeing highs around 102 today, which, in some areas, could potentially set record highs for certain locations."

He turned serious but still retained a wry smile. He subtly loosened his tie like a low-key Rodney Dangerfield. Maybe an attempt to win some connection with the audience.

"Be careful out there, folks! Drink plenty of H2O, wear a hat if you can, remember the sunscreen. Be careful about overloading electrical circuits when plugging in extra air conditioners, use pools if you have access to them, and make sure to check on your elderly friends and relatives."

Other than the hours at the bar, the regulars mostly operated on various independent schedules based on their preferences and responsibilities. It just so happened that everybody was simultaneously tuning into the weather report in some form. Don was changing the oil in his Mustang and had the broadcast on a tiny television in his garage, not paying attention to the picture but listening casually to the audio. Alonso was watching a live broadcast of the news on BrainSpot from his laptop in a lounge at the community college while he highlighted lines in a textbook. George watched from his couch with his feet propped up and a mug of lukewarm coffee sitting on his belly. Megan was half-listening to the television from her bedroom while she firmly tugged jean shorts up her son's chubby legs. Mo and Erin were at a convenience store, purchasing granola bars and to-go cups of tea. After paying, they both stood sipping their tea while watching the weather segment on the screen behind the counter that the cashier had been watching before they interrupted her. Nobody was in line behind them, so they could see the full report without moving away from the counter. They left as soon as it was over, as they were both pushing being late for their work start-time. Nick didn't like to listen to the television's blaring while he went over invoices, so it was turned on but muted in the corner of his home office. He took a break from the bills and read the closed captioning over the top of his reading glasses. Patrick could hear the weatherman's voice escaping from an open window while he skimmed the pool for leaves and bugs.

"Again, please be as careful as possible with the intense weather. I'm Richard Newton for News 8. Thanks for watching!"

Mancheville and the people in the surrounding area were indeed tired of hearing about the weather, nearly as much as they were tired of experiencing it. Pennsylvania was not supposed to be a place of relentless sun and triple-digit temperatures. The recent spell of excessive heat was no longer welcome to even the most summer-loving residents of Mancheville. It was so bad that strangers who had nothing to talk about were no longer even using the weather as a topic of conversation to avoid awkward silence.

The bar business is a fickle thing, and Nick never felt comfortable assuming that something he'd done was the reason for a spike in business. Experience teaches bar owners and managers—and frankly, any business owner—that putting too much stock in one marketing effort or protocol change because of temporary success can end up being detrimental. Even so, business had picked up in recent weeks, and Nick was silently praising himself for a couple of new drink specials he'd added during happy hour. The self-praise, of course, still came with his typical side of caution and humility, so he didn't toot his own horn to anybody else.

Nick took a moment to look over the current happy hour crowd. Samuel was seated in the spot he preferred. Alonso and Mo were sitting together at a table, which was unusual for them unless they were playing trivia. There were a few familiar couples that he gave friendly greetings to when they entered, despite not remembering their names. Breaking up the more familiar faces were two guys on business, one young and one old. Nick had a brief conversation with them, enough to know they were accountants conducting a scheduled routine audit on a local company. Nick couldn't remember their names, their company's name, or which place they were auditing, but he did remember that they were from the Cleveland area.

It was a pretty substantial crowd for being Thursday, still early in the evening, and hot as hell. Even though there were a fair amount of customers, Nick sensed something a tad bit off about the atmosphere in the room. He couldn't quite put his finger on it, but he wasn't going to spend too much time worrying about it. He'd rather keep working and just do his best to spread positive feelings when he could.

Samuel sat in the same general area that he typically sat, in the corner farthest away from the dining area. He was drinking one of the beers offered in Nick's recently launched happy hour special. In front of him were one neatly stacked pile of unscratched two-dollar lottery tickets, one messier pile of losing tickets, and a meager pile of winning tickets. With a quarter he'd selected because it was a bicentennial and seemed lucky, he slowly scratched at his remaining tickets, taking off tiny strips of pewter-colored material that turned into a fine ash-like dust. He wiped down the area with a napkin every two or three tickets to keep it relatively clean. Especially with Nick present, he didn't want to create a sloppy mess of ticket residue on the bar. He'd spoken only to Nick to say hello and the bartender to order since he'd arrived.

Alonso and Mo sat at a table in the dining area, although they were only drinking. It was unusual for them to sit at a table unless they were playing trivia. Neither spoke about it, but both seemed to understand that they should stay as far away from Samuel as possible. They didn't discuss their seat selection and reasons for it, but the online clash from the previous day was a conversation topic.

"So, that got pretty gnarly yesterday with Don. The post is no longer available. I think whoever runs the page just yanked it after you and Don went at it."

"I know, that's about as bad as it's ever gotten. I can usually talk myself out of getting involved in his posts. Just couldn't control myself. Dude drives me insane, man."

"I know. It's not like I like seeing his shit either. I just ignore it completely most of the time."

Alonso had no immediate answer and gave off just the hint of regret, although he had no interest in vocalizing it.

"You know I'll pretty much always defend you, but I have to admit you kind of started the personal stuff."

"I did but trashing my brother the way he did is so much worse than what I said about his ex-wife that he divorced forever ago."

"That's why Erin and I jumped in. It was totally wrong, bro. No argument there. I still can't believe he said that shit. Even if you start it, I still got you." Mo laughed, but it was more weary than merry.

"I appreciate it," Alonso answered feebly.

They were silent for nearly five minutes, and the bar was noticeably hushed despite the ample amount of people. It was quiet enough to hear the friction of Samuel's quarter on his tickets and the clinking of ice cubes every time somebody rearranged the contents of their cocktail with their straw. The only person making the occasional loud noise was another new bartender, a thirtyish male with a lean frame and a stylish haircut with an aggressive shave on one side entirely up to the natural part in his hair. He loaded the dishwasher and popped some wine corks, seeming somewhat oblivious to the muted ambiance.

Mo broke the silence first. "How has your brother been, anyway?"

Alonso only grunted at first but then answered, "About the same, I guess. Nothing different. Still with the same girl. He's still been cooking at whatever restaurant will put him on their schedule. He's pretty good at it, I guess, which is the only reason people still hire him. Every time he starts something new, there's a two to four-month time when he works his ass off and impresses management. As soon as he gets a few paychecks, he starts slipping. He only shows up half the time or disappears in the middle of his shift for an hour, and all kinds of other shit. Before ya know it, they can him. He can be a real idiot, it's true, but I still don't want anybody else pointing that out in a public comment section on BrainSpot."

"Have you talked to him anymore about rehab?"

Alonso recoiled at the question, clearly wanting to change the subject. "Thousand times, bro. All he does is mention that I still live at home and go out drinking all the time. He's got a point, but I'm in college and have a part-time job on campus that I show up to when I'm supposed to. I can't afford to move out until I'm done with school. And it'll probably be a few years after that, realistically."

"Not trashing him or anything, but he's just trying to make you seem bad to distract you and everybody else from his major problems. You're at the bar a lot, but you take care of your shit."

"I know, but it still makes it harder to confront him."

Mo knew better than to push Alonso any further and get him upset. He didn't want to wind him up and see him take it out on somebody at the bar and cause more stress than the BrainSpot debacle already had.

"How are your classes going?"

"Pretty good. I should get a B or better in all my classes except for math. I suck so bad at math. It's a probability and statistics course, so it's at least kind of interesting because it can be applied to real-life situations. But I'm still terrible at it. I have a nice professor, though; he's pretty cool about helping as long as you approach him and ask questions. I can't wait for it to be over, though. It's the last math class that I have to take. Thank freaking god."

"Glad to hear it's going well; I know you really started working hard the last couple of semesters."

"I think that's a nice way of saying I was a lazy asshole for a bunch of semesters before that," Alonso said with a grin.

Mo snickered and said back, "Well, yeah, you kinda were, but I seriously have noticed that you're putting in real effort now."

"Thanks, I'm just playing. I know you weren't trying to imply anything. How's your job going?"

Mo found himself surprised at the question. Alonso was his best friend, but he rarely asked Mo how he was doing or what was happening in his life. It was just his personality; he was typically too self-absorbed to ask about him or Erin.

"It's going well. It's a lower-level job in procurement, so I'm still learning a lot of stuff. I learned some of it in college, but it's different when you see it in the real business world."

"Awesome. I don't know if I understand everything about what you do, but I'm happy for you, bro. How's Erin's job? What does she do again? I forget."

"She works in HR at a steel plant. She likes it, but she'll probably move on in a couple of years. Both of us, actually. Both of our jobs are just entry-level, so if we want to make more money, we'll have to start looking at other companies' job openings. Or hope that people above us leave and create an opening at our current companies. We'll see what happens. We're just happy that we both got jobs in what we went to school for."

Alonso nodded approvingly and asked, "Where is Erin anyway?"

"She had to stop at her parents' house. They cleaned out their garage and found some stuff they wanted her to go through before they started throwing things away. She's gonna meet us later at The Night's Quest."

"Cool. We can have one or two more here and then head over. Unless we need to go sooner."

"Nope, we can hang out a little here. She texted me a few minutes ago and said she'd be at her parents' for at least an hour more."

When Don entered the pub, Alonso noticed him but had no visible reaction. Don saw him in his peripheral but didn't turn to look at him. Instead, he made his way to the stool beside Samuel, who put his forearm on the bar and swiped his lottery ticket piles away from the spot where Don was going to sit. Don ordered a beer from the new bartender. When it arrived, he took a short swig and exhaled loudly, after he swallowed.

"Evening, Sammy."

"Evening, how's Don doing today?"

"I'm okay. Did a little work on the car this morning before it got too hot, then I just laid on my ass inside in the A.C. until I came here. How goes it with you?"

"I'd be doing better if I could hit something decent on one of these tickets. Only got eight dollars of my money back so far."

"Never liked those damn things. Unless it's a poker game, I don't care to gamble my hard-earned money."

"I like 'em; it's entertainment for me."

"Whatever, it's your money."

"Hey, did anything else happen with your best buddy and his friend over there?" Samuel gestured with his head towards the table where Alonso and Mo were seated.

"No, I can't even get to the post anymore. They removed it or something."

"That might be for the better. It was getting pretty bad."

"Little prick has a smart mouth in person, and he's even worse when he's typing. Big tough guy when he can hide in his mom's basement and insult me."

"He sure can be a miserable little bastard. I don't blame ya for going after him."

"I don't know why he thinks he can just leave his rude little remarks on something that I posted and not get anything back. And he's the one that turned it into something personal. I'm getting sick and tired of..." Don stopped what he was saying when he saw George and Patrick coming around the bar towards them. He wasn't sure if they'd seen the whole thing on BrainSpot. Patrick doesn't even have an account. If he'd seen it, it would have been because his wife showed him. There was a chance that George was aware of it, but Don didn't want to discuss the incident in front of him. If it could blow over without George knowing, he'd prefer it that way.

"Hey, boys, ya leave any beer for us?" questioned Patrick with a grin.

"They have a barrel in the back for you that should last you until midnight," Don retorted.

"Hey, Pat. Hey, George. Staying cool out there?"

"I can't believe this weather. Patrick's pool was a lifesaver today."

Don shook his head like he was a disappointed father, and the weather was his child. "Yeah, I almost came over, but I couldn't convince myself to step outside for a second during the hottest part of the day. Just sat like a lump in the air conditioning." As he was speaking, he caught Alonso's staring eyes from across the room. The friendly smile he had on his face for George and Patrick immediately disappeared. He only kept eye contact for a moment, but it reignited his anger from the night before. Even so, he was determined to resist the urge to act on his irritation.

Even though he hadn't been paying much attention to the atmosphere earlier, the new bartender eventually started to feel the underlying tension in the pub. He went to the supply cabinet for a roll of paper towels. He noticed that Nick was standing nearby, hovering over his desk with a pen in his mouth, looking like he was profoundly contemplating something on the various pieces of paper spread over the desktop.

"Hey, Nick. Sorry to bother you, but can I ask you something?"

Nick pulled the pen from between his teeth and replied, "No problem at all. What's on your mind?"

"Is there any reason that the customers might not like me? Am I doing anything wrong that you've noticed?"

"I don't think so; it seems like you're doing a great job for just starting. Why do you ask?"

"I don't know; it just seems heavy out there. Everybody has been pretty polite for the most part, but something seems off."

"I have to be honest; I noticed it too. They're nicer to me because they know me, but I agree that something feels wrong. I don't know. Some folks out there don't always get along with each other, but it does seem like something more than that. I wish I had an answer, but I don't. Some days it's just a 'misery loves company' kind of day, I guess. Don't worry, though; it's not you. Just keep doing what you're doing. It's definitely not you. I'm confident of that."

"Thanks, Nick."

"You bet. Worst case scenario, if you have a problem, just find me, and I'll take care of it. You'll be fine, though. Just get out there and pour some refills before the natives get restless." They both laughed, and Nick gave him a pat on the back like a coach motivating his player before sending him back on the field.

Alonso stared at the ceiling, possibly holding back tears. His conversation with Mo had again steered back to Don and BrainSpot. "I just get so frustrated with people like him who think that to be a good person, your life has to be exactly like theirs. Like there is some blueprint to being a real American that you have to follow or you're not acceptable. It's such bullshit."

"I feel the same way sometimes. I just try not to think about it too much, especially the things people say online. I mean, I've had to deal with a lot of shit because of the way I look. I've been called a terrorist and a towelhead. That one's especially weird because I literally don't wear anything on my head. I don't even wear baseball hats too often. It can be hard to understand where my place is. I just try to remember that, really, most people have nothing against me and don't automatically assume I'm a suicide bomber because I have a Middle Eastern complexion. The loudest people talking about anything are usually the last ones to listen to."

"I've seriously thought about just closing my BrainSpot account for a little bit to stop getting so pissed off on a daily basis. I wish I could just calmly read things and not react, but it's like I get in this zone where I'm not even in control of myself. I might take a break soon."

"Do what you have to do. I won't talk you out of it." Mo couldn't help but notice that even though Alonso was talking reasonably, he was looking across the bar at the same time, his eyes boring holes into Don's head.

Don could sense that Alonso was looking his way again, but he kept his attention on Samuel, who was discussing how he stopped in at Hank's the night before. "Did she mention me at all?"

By the look on Samuel's face, it was clear that Megan had not brought up Don. He tried his best not to explicitly say so, offering, "I went by myself, and she did ask me where the rest of the guys were, which certainly includes you. I really think she was mostly referring to you."

"Yeah, sure. I know I'm a dumbass for even thinking she'd ask about me."

"C'mon, don't be so hard on yourself."

"I'm just lonely. A man needs a woman around. I haven't even had a girlfriend in a decade. It's pathetic."

"Well, you have your freedom. No wife to answer to or nag you."

"I've had enough freedom. I'm ready to move on, even if it comes with some nagging."

The sound of George and Patrick's voices got louder as they returned from the dartboard in a small back room where they had shot a game. Patrick was trying to convince George that he owed him a drink because he beat him, but George was calmly insisting that Patrick had counted his points wrong. Both got tired of arguing and joined Samuel and Don.

"George said he's going to walk over to The Night's Quest awhile and get something to eat. I'm going to get one more here and leave after that. How about you guys?"

"I believe I'll do the same as you, Pat," answered Don.

Samuel decided to do the same and replied, "Yep, me too."

"We'll see ya over there in a little while, George."

One of the things that George had to get used to after Anna passed away was eating alone in public. Decades of always having a partner to dine with had left him very unfamiliar with doing anything else. On the rare times that Anna wasn't around, he either ate at home or made plans to meet somebody at a restaurant or bar. Once she passed, though, there were times that he just didn't feel like eating in the house, and he didn't want to be a bother constantly calling people for dinner dates. He gradually got more used to it, although it still felt odd at times. It was one of the reasons that he started attending the bars more often after her passing. More of a reason than any solace he got from drinking alcohol.

Even when not joining a friend, eating at the bar still felt like dining with somebody else. Even an empty bar has a bartender. George wasn't even a big talker, although he was happy to engage if somebody else opened the conversation. But a bartender, or a patron five seats down, or a waitress on break, was at least a presence. In a restaurant, a party of one seems more sad or suspicious. It always seems like the person is somehow throwing off the balance of the room. Is he stalking somebody? Undercover cop on a case? Is she waiting for somebody who is just really, really late? Did he just get dumped? Is she such a horrific bitch that she can't even get anybody to eat a meal with her? Is he mentally ill and insists on eating in solitude?

The truth is that those questions are rarely on peoples' minds. Most people probably pay no mind to somebody dining alone. But it's hard not to feel like all of those things are running through people's heads as soon as you enter a restaurant and tell the hostess that it will just be a table for one.

George had a cup of chicken noodle soup and a small salad to start his meal. He opted for the vinaigrette dressing because it was healthier than Ranch or Thousand Island. He drank an iced tea while he ate, sweetening it lightly with just half a pack of sugar before squeezing some lemon juice into the glass and finally letting the lemon wedge fall into the tea and rest amongst the ice cubes. He'd switch to beer after his meal. He chose pork chops as his entrée with broccoli and sweet potato on the side.

As he made his way through his soup and salad, he noticed some faces of folks who had thrown in their two cents on the BrainSpot comment threads the night before. Betty Anders, an octogenarian grandmother who was still spry enough to be a crossing guard at the elementary school, was sitting on one side of the dining room. She'd learned how to use a computer at the library and had a BrainSpot account that she used occasionally. She happened to see Don and Alonso's back-and-forth and decided to leave a comment in support of Don. Older than Betty by just one year at eighty-six, Sarah Ross had learned computer basics in the same class as her. She'd added a comment in support of Alonso after Don had disparaged his brother. Both Betty and Sarah sat with their husbands, and George couldn't help but feel like they were scowling at each other periodically. He swore he could feel some of the same tension in The Night's Quest as was present at the pub. He wasn't sure if it was real or if he imagined it.

"Hi, George, how are you?"

He stopped examining Betty and Sarah and turned his attention to where the voice was coming from. Erin stood smiling beside one of the chairs at George's table. He motioned for her to take a seat and returned her smile. She gently pulled the seat out, careful not to let the legs scrape on the floor and make an obnoxious noise, as they sometimes did. She rested her forearms on the edge of the table, waiting for George to respond.

"I'm doing well, Erin, and you?"

"Pretty good. I just had to work late to get some paperwork done, so I'm happy to be done. I'm starving."

"Well, I don't have much left. I wish I had an appetizer or something to share. Not that exciting, but you're welcome to some broccoli or a bite from the other half of my pork chop. I haven't eaten off of either one."

Erin giggled and said, "That's sweet of you, George, but I can wait and order my own dinner. Mo and Alonso should be here soon to join me."

"Oh, I just saw them at the pub. I didn't get a chance to say hello. Are they doing okay?"

"Yeah, they're okay. Alonso is... Alonso." She smiled uneasily and added, "I'm not sure if you've seen it, but he and Don got into it on some posts on some random BrainSpot pages. I can't remember what they were." George hoped he didn't look nervous or guilty. He shrugged like he didn't know what she was talking about and let her continue. "It was just a stupid thing, but a few people from town got involved. Alonso and Don both said some pretty horrible things to each other. Mo and I even added some comments. I don't know why; we rarely get involved in crap like that. People got defensive, and it was so unpleasant."

"Oh jeez, sorry to hear that. I talked to Don for a little at the pub, but he didn't mention it." George felt bad about lying, but it certainly didn't seem like the time or place to admit that he was not only aware of it but also partially at fault for it happening.

"Anyway, I don't want to bother you anymore. I'm gonna grab a seat at the bar and wait for the other two."

"Not a bother at all. Enjoy your dinner."

She left, and George returned to eating, alternating between bites of broccoli florets and pork. Only a few minutes later, Mo and Alonso entered. They saw George and gave him a small wave before scanning the room and finding Erin at the bar.

They sat on either side of her, and both began perusing the menu. Erin already had the idea to order several appetizers, and all share them. Mo and Alonso were on board with the plan. When they got the bartender's attention, they ordered jalapeno poppers, French fries, mozzarella sticks, and a quesadilla with salsa and sour cream. Erin collected the menus and passed them to the bartender.

"I'm starving. I can't wait to eat."

"You and Mo could have gotten something at the pub; I wouldn't have cared."

"It's okay; I only really just got super hungry when we left."

"How was work, babe?"

"Long and tedious, but I got everything finished. They really can't prepare you in college for the amount of paperwork that needs to be done in human resources. Of course, I'm lowest on the totem pole, so the most boring stuff gets passed on to me. It's not even hard, just a bunch of signatures and dates and checkmarks. But it sucks."

"Glad you're done for the night." Mo and Erin embraced and gave each other a small peck on the cheek.

"Well, aren't you two just the freaking cutest!" Alonso said play-fully before cocking his head and sucking on the straw resting in the mojito that Erin had ordered for him before they arrived. "Thanks for the drink, BABE." He emphasized the last word while grandly rolling his eyes.

"What, are you jealous of me or something? You just got two hours alone with Mo. Back off, buddy!" She pulled a fork from the wrapped silverware and held it like a dagger over Alonso's chest. Mo lightly grabbed the fork from Erin's fist grip and laid it further down the bar where she couldn't reach it. Erin and Alonso laughed and gently clinked their drinks together lightheartedly.

Mo rolled his eyes with a small smile and remarked simply, "Weir-dos."

They discussed a paper that Alonso had to finish by the end of the week. Erin reflected on her essays in college and mentioned that she had no confidence in her writing. She gave Alonso some advice on how to break up the writing and make it easier on himself. He seemed to be paying attention, didn't say much, and even made eye contact and listened attentively. Mo was impressed with his friend and thought maybe Alonso was turning a corner with some of his anxiety and impulsive behavior. Maybe the BrainSpot ugliness had triggered a change.

Almost on cue, Mo saw that Don, Samuel, and Patrick had entered and joined George at his table. Their drinks were fresh, and they seemed to be having a pleasant conversation amongst themselves. Mo hoped that Alonso wouldn't see them and interrupt his engagement with Erin's conversation. But he glanced where Mo was looking and saw the table of four.

"Just don't even look over there."

Mo was surprised again when Alonso obeyed without question. Erin gave a quick look over her shoulder and immediately realized what Mo was talking about.

"I'm doing my best, but it might get harder if I keep drinking these mojitos."

Mo jokingly punched Alonso's chin in dramatic slow-motion fashion. Alonso didn't react except to let one side of his lip curl up, giving the hint of a smile. It became clear after some time that Alonso wasn't going to do anything that might start some shit at The Night's Quest. But he did keep drinking mojitos.

Andy sat his order pad on the small table beside an ashtray. He grabbed the cigarette that the bartender held out for him. He snatched it greedily and started to light it with the lighter he picked up from beside the ashtray.

"Ah, ah, ah. What the hell?"

Andy grabbed him with one arm around his waist and kissed him on the neck.

"That's better. You know I need a little appreciation before you smoke my cigarettes."

"Jeez, you're so needy. You're as bad as those regulars in there."

"Hey, I'm a bitch, but those people relish getting drunk and starting drama even more than I do. They're not as catty or loud as me when I get nasty, but Jesus, do they love to hate each other."

The only place they were allowed to smoke was in a little hidden alcove outside the kitchen. That was perfectly fine with them because it gave them a chance to show affection to each other without Andy worrying that any customers who were also his grandmother's friends would report something back to her. He was twenty-seven, so he was free to do what he wanted, and his grandmother didn't even care about him being gay, but he didn't want her friends discussing it in detail with her, with their air of fake concern that was just a front for being gossipy. Besides, Robby was in the closet still anyway, so he wouldn't rub Andy's shoulders or embrace him and certainly wouldn't kiss him. Not in public, anyway.

"Seriously, they all go to the same places as each other at least four nights a week, but three of those nights somebody is pissed at somebody else. I don't even get it. Why don't they just go to different places if they despise each other so much?"

"It's Mancheville, not Manhattan. They can't just choose a different part of town and have hundreds of other bars to go to. Anyway, listen to you. Every time you go out to clubs, all you do is get in fights with your queen friends."

"I'm gay; I live to be sassy. And I don't do it a bunch of nights a week. Only on special occasions do I let my inner diva out!"

"I know, I know. Most of the time, you're just regular ol' Robert. I drove by your parents' house the other day and saw you helping your dad fix his Jeep. You even had your tight, dirty jeans on and oil smudges on your cheeks like you were posing for some beefcake calendar." Andy stubbed out his cigarette and added, "Adorable."

"My dad would love to hear that that is what you got from us replacing an alternator," Robby said sarcastically.

Andy laughed heartily and then said, "Okay, I gotta get back to it. You probably have some waiting customers too."

"I'm sure Alonso needs his next mojito. He's a cute little thing, but man, he can be a pain in the ass."

"I haven't served him often, but the few times I have confirmed that you ain't lyin'."

By ten o'clock, everybody who was drinking in a bar in Mancheville had found their way to Hank's. The only exceptions were Nick, who was cleaning the speakers at The Mancheville Pub while sipping red wine, and Andy and Robby, who were cleaning up alone at The Night's Quest and drinking Tom Collins cocktails while doing so.

Both establishments had closed for the night when people started migrating to Hank's. If they hadn't closed, some customers might have returned. Hank's air conditioning was on the fritz and was periodically going out of service. Initially, it would stop working for only a few minutes before kicking back on with a blast of hot air followed by fresh, cool air. That became five-minute breakdowns, which eventually turned into the air conditioning being down more often than it was operating.

For some reason, nobody wanted to surrender to the heat and just go home for the night. In an act of collective defiance towards the weather, the defective air conditioning, and all kinds of other shit pissing them off, the bar stayed full, even as it got hotter and steamier. Samuel and Patrick took their brave stand to another level by continuing to chain-smoke cigarettes despite there being minimal air movement in the room. The fans were working, but only at their normal slow pace that didn't move much air. An abnormally substantial cloud of smoke hung over the bar area, and it seemed to grow larger every minute. Several people were shooting them dirty, disgusted looks, even some people who customarily smoked but were abstaining from the already thick atmosphere. Either the smoke cloud was too thick to see the glares, or they just didn't bother the puffing duo.

Megan was among the people who didn't care for the smoking, but she decided to remain quiet about it instead of causing a rift. If anybody complained to her, perhaps she would have a conversation with the guys, but she wouldn't do it for her own purposes. Her only way of passive-aggressively showing her displeasure was to violently wave the smoke away from her face every time she brought them fresh drinks. Sadly, they didn't pick up on the meaning of her gesture.

Alonso had been well-behaved, particularly by his standards, and especially for how many mojitos that he'd sent to his stomach. He had remained mostly quiet except for conversing with Mo and Erin, but he was sufficiently intoxicated. He was visibly sweating and becoming more agitated as the heat rose and the smoke cloud expanded. Loud enough for most of the bar to hear, he suddenly sprang up from his stool and proclaimed. "Mo, I need to grab something from my backpack in your car. Let me have your keys." Mo seemed perplexed but opened the carabiner that was attached to one of his belt loops and handed them over. Alonso grabbed them and went outside without another word.

Don eyed Alonso suspiciously during his outburst and as he went out the door. It was strange, and Don couldn't conceive what he could possibly need outside. A dry new shirt to replace the sweaty one? A comb to fix his hair that had become sloppy after dozens of swipes to remove sweat from his forehead? Don couldn't help himself from becoming increasingly concerned about the sudden trip outside. Even when he was drawn back into conversation with Samuel, Patrick, and George, his eyes remained locked on the door, waiting for Alonso to return.

Meanwhile, George had barely paid attention to Alonso. His antics didn't come as a surprise to him anymore. He was instead concerned with a minor pain growing in his stomach. He hoped it wasn't undercooked pork, causing a disturbance in his belly that might develop into something even worse. The heat and smoke were not helping. Added to that were his sporadic feelings of guilt about the BrainSpot issue, which evoked physical pangs of discomfort alongside whatever else was happening in his internal organs.

"Excuse me, fellas. I'm going to use the restroom. Be right back." He tried not to show any evidence of his pain. He slid off his stool and started for the men's room.

Alonso re-entered the bar area with a goofy, wicked smile on his face, looking almost triumphant for some reason. He lifted his right hand, and a black object was visible, gripped in his tightened fist. With his eyes on Megan's back, he pointed the item at her and silently waited for her to turn around.

Don had taken his eyes off the door when George interrupted his conversation and mentioned that he was going to the restroom. He was staring at his beer, forgetting to keep watch over the door. He was instantly alert again when he heard Megan scream from across the room. Through the heavy smoke, he saw Alonso pointing something at her and reacted. He grabbed his small .38 Special from his pocket, aimed quickly, and fired a shot towards Alonso.

George had just passed Alonso on his way to the restroom, not paying attention to anything going on at the bar. He collapsed before he made it to where Mo and Erin were seated, wondering if his stomach pain had been something more insidious than he'd imagined. He went into a fetal position on the floor, and everything went completely silent to him. There was pressure in his side that turned into intense, searing pain. Eventually, he lost consciousness.

Don, standing rigid in a state of shock, dropped his gun onto the floor. It clattered loudly and awkwardly and was the only sound in the silence after the gunshot. When everybody got over the ringing in their ears, there was a chaotic mess of shouting and screaming. Don felt the blood leave his body when he realized that Alonso was not holding a gun as he'd initially thought. He let Patrick and Samuel secure him tightly without a fight. Megan jumped over the bar and pushed everyone away from the area where the gun was, already dialing 911 on her cell phone and holding it to her ear.

Alonso also stood in a state of shock, as unmoving as a statue. In his hand, he still held the little black battery-operated personal fan that he'd brought in and jokingly pointed at Megan like a pistol. The small, harmless blades were still spinning on it, disrupting the dense haze of smoke above the bar.

CHAPTER NINETEEN

George awoke briefly to almost complete darkness, not knowing where he was. Even in his sleepy haze, he could tell he wasn't at home, but the few objects he could identify gave him no clues about his location. A digital clock with red letters read 3:41. A medium-size flat-screen television on the wall was turned on but only displayed a glowing gray screen because the cable had been turned off. He could see what looked to be chairs but couldn't bend forward enough to see them clearly. He heard some steady beeps and boops that were familiar sounds he'd heard before, but he was still too out-of-sorts to understand what they were. He laid his head back on the hot pillow, too tired to worry about flipping it to the cooler side. It was the first time that he'd felt even a moment of actual consciousness in over a day. The pain medications they'd given him were strong and incapacitated him for some time. He dozed off again, still requiring a few more hours of sleep to rid himself of the grogginess.

As it turned out, George had only been experiencing gas and acid reflux when he'd stood up to go to the bathroom at Hank's. Those ailments ended up being the least of his worries. Of more concern was the fact that Don's bullet had missed Alonso and instead found the side of George's torso. It only grazed him, so he was going to be okay, but it was still a major shock to the body. Especially a seventy-year-old body in mediocre shape at best.

The police arrested Don without any struggle or problem. Everyone at Hank's was reeling from the shooting, including Alonso, of course. Everyone assumed he would react to the incident with a furious rage and a vow to get back at Don. But it wasn't the same as an argument or a battle with typed words on a comment thread. The realness seemed to shake him up so much that he didn't react in the way generally expected of him. He seemed to have almost no immediate reaction.

After the E.M.T. staff took George away to the hospital in an ambulance, the police took witness statements and collected personal information before sending the bar patrons home. Megan was permitted to stay during the scene investigation. However, she had to wait until it was finished until she touched or cleaned anything. She was disturbed by the whole thing but maintained her usual strong demeanor.

Patrick and Samuel left Hank's as soon as possible and immediately went to the hospital to find out George's condition. When they were told he was stable but couldn't see any visitors yet, they both went home to get some sleep.

Don spent thirty hours in a jail cell, waiting for the judge to set his bail. When it was finally set at $50,000, he contacted a lawyer and then a bail bondsman. He agreed to terms with the first bondsman he talked to, and less than an hour after signing the paperwork, was free to return to his home and await trial. He did so and purposely avoided talking to anybody in Mancheville. Don carried a heavy combination of shame, guilt, and embarrassment about what he'd done and even feared somewhat for his safety. The phone and the door were left unanswered. He completely refrained from using Brain-Spot. In fact, he decided not to get on the internet at all indefinitely.

Around nine o'clock, George woke up again, this time sensing that somebody else was in the room. At first, when he sat up, his eyes were still blurry, and he thought it was Ethan standing beside his hospital bed. He was astonished when he realized that it was his daughter. She looked quite a bit like Ethan, especially with his blurry vision. In the last two decades, he had barely spoken to Elizabeth since an unfortunate, intense disagreement that they'd had before she was married and before Ethan was born. She would only talk to him to let him know when she moved or something of interest happened with Ethan. Elizabeth spoke more to Anna, but not much more. Anything Anna learned, she passed on to George, but it was usually vague and impersonal information. They communicated only by phone or email.

At a young age, she had let Ethan choose if he wanted to have a relationship with George and Anna. He decided that it was something he wanted, so Elizabeth let it happen. She still had a grudge against her father but did not despise him enough to prohibit a relationship between him and his grandson. George had felt quite a bit of anger and bitterness for the first couple years of their disconnection, but that morphed into only sadness and regret for the rest of the years. Even so, he couldn't raise the courage or swallow his pride enough to convince himself to reach out and reconnect in a real way.

"Wow, hi, Elizabeth."

"Hi, Dad. Are you feeling okay? I couldn't believe it when I heard the news."

"I'm feeling fine. Definitely sore, but they've had me on medication that has me feeling no pain, and I've been pretty zonked out for the most part."

"Well, I'm glad you're not feeling too much pain."

"Thanks; I'm very glad to see you, despite the circumstances."

"Well, when Ethan told me what happened, I felt like I had to pay you a visit."

Ethan was actually with Elizabeth, but he wanted to hear George's reaction to his mom before making himself known. He came out of the bathroom with a tepid smile, happy that they both seemed pleased to see each other in person but not trusting that it would last. He went to the opposite side of the bed from his mother and gave George a very, very careful hug. George rubbed his back lovingly. Elizabeth put her hand on George's shoulder gently, leaving it there for a few minutes while searching his eyes. He grabbed her wrist sweetly but winced in pain from the movement. She removed her hand and used it to adjust his pillow so his head would be centered on it.

Elizabeth updated George on her job, the new car she'd recently purchased, how she was dealing with Ethan being in college, and other details about her life. It was nothing Earth-shattering, but George was enjoying just hearing her voice in person. Two decades was a long time, and brief phone conversations were simply not the same as face-to-face interaction. He said little while she talked, speaking only to affirm that he was still listening. Even when she spoke in detail about quitting her spin class and joining a yoga class instead, he listened like it was the most engaging story in the world. Elizabeth, with help from Ethan, eventually got around to discussing the incident at Hank's before they were interrupted by a soft knock on the doorframe.

A few seconds later, Alonso entered timidly, unsure if he might wake George up or interrupt a nurse conducting a medical procedure. Seeing that neither was a possibility, he straightened up and stepped further into the room with a little more confidence. He looked exhausted but smiled at the three of them, greeting Ethan by name since he knew him from the concert. Ethan introduced his mother to Alonso, and they shook hands politely.

Elizabeth picked up her purse from a chair and said, "How about we let Alonso and George talk while we go grab something to eat, Ethan?"

"Sounds great; I'm hungry."

"Oh, you don't have to leave. I'm just gonna have a short visit with George."

Elizabeth waved him off. "No, it's okay. I'm hungry and need to walk around for a little bit."

They exited the room, and George was left alone with Alonso.

"Well, Don and I always keep it exciting at Hank's, huh?"

George laughed as lightly as he could, not wanting to disturb his damaged side again. "You sure do! I just heard everything my daughter and grandson know about what happened. I barely knew anything. Before I passed out, I vaguely recall knowing that I'd heard something that sounded like a gunshot. The last thing I remember is feeling like shit and getting up to visit the restroom. Everything after that is just a foggy blur."

"To be honest, it's a little foggy for me too. I was wasted. I wasn't blackout, so I do remember the basics of what happened. It's not clear, though."

"I doubt that it is for anybody. It's just so crazy."

"Oh, I almost forgot; I have something for you." Alonso stepped out of the room and came back in with a bouquet that had a small 'Get Well!' card stuck in the top. He pulled the card out and handed it to George before walking around his bed and placing the flowers on the window ledge. George checked out the front of the card's colorful design and then flipped it over. On the back, someone had scrawled: 'Heal quickly so you can have a beer with us again soon! From Mo, Erin, and Alonso.' He felt a rush of tears but blinked them away. "How are you, Alonso? This is quite a situation to process."

"I'm okay. Still just shocked as hell."

"I don't blame you. I'm kind of feeling that way myself. From what my family tells me, the consensus is that Don was sincerely acting in a protective, defensive manner. It certainly doesn't justify anything. I know for a fact that he has a concealed carry permit, but even with that, he really shouldn't be carrying while drinking. I don't know if it's something he did all the time, or if he just started doing it, or if it was just a one-time thing, and he forgot he had it."

"I don't know if I'm nuts or what. That guy has always gotten under my skin, even when he did just the smallest thing. Now, when he does something that I should be unbelievably pissed about, I don't have that anger. It doesn't make sense. Maybe that'll change eventually. I mean, I don't want it to, but maybe once everything sets in, it will happen."

"Don screwed up big time, and he deserves a consequence. But honestly, I don't seem to feel much anger towards him either. I mostly just feel lucky for both of us that I wasn't fatally injured. It could be much worse for him; he might have been facing prison for the rest of his life. He's looking at something serious, but he'll get out with plenty of years of his life left. I assume anyway. I'm no lawyer. And obviously, I'm fortunate not just to be alive, but to escape from this with only a minor wound."

"I still think he's an idiot, but damn, I didn't think he had it in him to actually use a gun when he felt like he needed to defend somebody. It was misguided, but I have to give him some kind of weird credit for that. As strange as that might sound. I'm really sorry you were hurt because of it, though."

"I guess what you're saying kind of sums of knowing Don." George laughed, trying as much as he could to keep it to a light chuckle. "And don't feel bad. I know you were just joking around with Megan. Maybe a stupid thing to do, but it was far from malicious. It's nice of you to visit and bring flowers."

"Not that I wouldn't have visited anyway, but I was already here for something else. So, visiting you is no trouble."

George wondered if that meant Alonso was here for something involved with his college nursing program. Perhaps he knew somebody who was at the hospital. He knew that if Alonso left out the information, it probably meant that he didn't want to talk about it, so he didn't press him on it. They spoke a bit longer about more benign topics than the shooting until Alonso finally said that he had to leave. Not sure how to give George a physical salutation and feeling like a wave wasn't quite enough when the man had taken a bullet meant for him, he gave George an awkward but tender handshake.

When Alonso was gone, he used the remote to find a rerun of yesterday's Phillies game. He laid back in the bed for comfort but was now thoroughly awake and coherent. He couldn't help but think, yet again, about BrainSpot and how he'd played a part in building the resentment and stress that had led up to the shooting. He felt guilty, but he certainly didn't feel like getting shot was a fair consequence of his actions. He tried to run the whole scene at Hank's over in his head, but it was all still incomplete and frustratingly unclear.

A half-hour later, in the bottom of the sixth of the Phillies game replay, Elizabeth and Ethan entered his room while conversing about the coffee quality in the cafeteria. He claimed it was terrible, while she said it was pretty good for a hospital cafeteria—at least a seven out of ten in the grand scheme of things. Ethan said it was both bitter and watered down, which is a terrible combination that should never happen. If it was bitter, it should at least be strong and not diluted. Elizabeth contended that he was so obsessed with Starbucks that he would trash anything else and defend the coffee giant no matter what. They both laughed at the silliness of their argument before turning their attention to George.

"Hey, Dad, still doing well?"

"I am. So, you guys checked out the cafeteria?"

"Yep, just got some bagels and coffee. Excellent coffee, I highly recommend it!" Elizabeth elbowed Ethan in the ribs.

"I gotta say, I'm pretty hungry myself. Will they give me lunch?"

"Sorry, they asked me about breakfast, but I wasn't sure how long you were going to sleep. You seemed to be out pretty good. Figured we wouldn't waste the food."

"Not a problem. I'm hungry, but I'll survive until lunch. Do I have to order it or something?"

"Someone from dietary will come around and ask if you want lunch. Maybe give you some options to choose from. I'm not certain about that. Do you need a snack to tide you over?"

"No, no, I can wait for lunch."

"Should we leave a note, or something, in case you fall asleep again?"

"I'm awake now. I think the painkillers have worn off, and I've certainly had plenty of rest. I'll probably be watching the end of this Phillies game or Sportscenter when they come around."

"Okay, great. Ethan has to head out. He has a class later and still has some work that he has to do in the library, so he's gotta get back to campus."

"Sorry that I can't stay longer, grandpa. Hope you're feeling better and get back on your feet soon."

"I'm sure I will. I already think the wound is starting to heal. Love you, Ethan."

"Love you too!" He gave George a timid hug and pulled back quickly, saying, "Let me know if you need anything or if something needs to be done at the house. I'm sure I can find time if the grass needs mowed or something."

"You're the best. I'm guessing somebody in town will handle that for me, but if they don't, I'll call you. Go take care of your school-work."

Ethan exchanged goodbyes with George and Elizabeth and left. They sat in silence until neither of them could hear the squeak of his sneakers in the hallway. Elizabeth was now a grown woman with a hint of wrinkles and chubbiness that inevitably comes with growing older. She worked out and was in pretty good shape for a woman in her forties but did have stubborn areas on her side and arms where age and a deteriorating metabolism were winning. But that's not what George saw. Nor did he see a strong-willed nineteen-year-old, the last version of her that he'd seen in person. Instead, he couldn't help himself from seeing eight-year-old Elizabeth when she'd broken her ankle. Provoked by the medical environment surrounding them, he remembered the terrible feeling of seeing his daughter lying in a hos-pital bed, crying more from the scariness of being entrapped in the hospital than the injury itself. He tried to push the memory from his brain and be sure to address his daughter like the woman she had become and not a vulnerable grade-schooler.

"Well, Dad. I'm here. I don't want to bother you while you're still in the hospital, but we have some things to discuss if this isn't the last time we see each other for another twenty years. Pleasantries and life updates are fine and all, but they're easy to talk about."

George nodded. "I have no problem talking here. It's not like I have a whole lot to do. I've missed you very much."

"I've missed you too. Things just get to a point where getting through life takes over, and the idea of patching things up becomes an afterthought. Months become years, and years become decades. I feel so ridiculous that it's been this long."

"It's more of a parent's responsibility to reconnect, Liz." She was very briefly surprised at him using the nickname that he'd always used for her growing up. When he hadn't used it to greet her initially, she wasn't sure if he'd ever address her by that name again. It was a bit of a test to see how she'd react. He was pleased when she didn't seem to scoff or recoil when he used the name. "Life takes on a whole different meaning when you realize your parents are just people. Sure, when you're a teenager, you might think your parents are wrong about everything, but you look at them as these beings who don't understand emotion and struggle; robotic authoritarians who don't think and feel like you. When you get a little older, things can become very strained when you suddenly realize that your parents are just grinding along like everybody else, trying to figure out what the hell it's all about. It's not a comfortable thing to come to grips with that as a young adult. You're smart, so you realized it early on. I was, and still am, as flawed as the next guy, and I demonstrated that by not being strong enough to initiate peace between us sooner."

"Do you remember what caused our fight?"

"Of course, I do. How could I forget?" He did remember but was reluctant to say it out loud.

"When I got pregnant during the summer after high school, I had never seen you so angry with me. It was with a guy that I met at the beach. I'd been on birth control for years already, but you didn't know. Mom knew but kept it secret. She knew it would be difficult for you to understand all of the complicated reasons that women take birth control beyond the obvious reasons. Anyway, something happened. I don't know if I got sloppy with taking my pills or what."

George moved the head portion of his bed up straighter and turned the television off, wanting to pay his full attention to Elizabeth.

"You didn't talk to me for days until I finally let loose on you about how it was my body, and I was the only one that would make the decisions about what I did with it. While true, I was just pissed off at your reaction and couldn't admit that getting pregnant at that time and in that manner was a mistake. It was, and I knew it. I was immature and scared, so my behavior wasn't rational.

George felt his face become flush, and his eyes became wet. Regardless of the circumstances, he was incredibly ashamed that he hadn't just calmed his daughter down and helped her in whatever way she needed to stay healthy and safe. It sounded so easy now.

"I moved out and went to live with Tara, a friend who'd graduated a couple of years ahead of me and had her own apartment. I was able to arrange healthcare to get through the pregnancy. I never told you this, but I decided to go forward with the pregnancy. The father even made a halfhearted offer to help with the baby, although I didn't put much stock in it. I knew that I was capable of raising the child myself if I had to. So, I was able to find assistance for young, pregnant women, found myself a job, and thought I was ready for whatever happened. Unfortunately, I had a miscarriage in the seventh week of my pregnancy. All of that preparation, only to lose the baby."

George closed his eyes to avoid completely sobbing. "I'm so sorry that happened, Liz. So sorry. We never knew anything about it. Nobody ever told us anything. You never seemed to want to talk on the phone for more than three minutes, much less have a deep conversation about what happened with your pregnancy. We didn't assume anything. I don't think either of us ever stopped wondering, but we did eventually stop talking about it. It was just such a painful thing to discuss. Maybe I'm wrong, though. Did your mother know about it, and you didn't want her to tell me?"

"No, no, she didn't. I hate that I kept both of you in the dark, but it was just so hard to talk about over the phone. I was on such an emotional rollercoaster. I guess avoiding you two was what I had to do, so I didn't become completely overwhelmed. So, I changed plans again. I enrolled in college and switched to a part-time job. I met Benjamin on campus when he was in his last semester, and we fell in love immediately. He had his head on straight and already had a real job lined up for when he was done with school. Once he started that, he got an apartment near campus, and I moved in. Soon after, we got married at the courthouse. Less than a year after that, Ethan came along. The rest is history."

It was both sad and satisfying to hear her speak about those years shrouded in confusion and mystery for George. He already knew some of the details that she'd mentioned, but he was more than happy to listen to everything explained clearly and succinctly, right from her mouth. "Thanks, Liz. It means a lot that you'll talk to me. You certainly don't owe me an explanation about anything."

"Maybe not, but I handled things pretty poorly on my end. I have to acknowledge my part in our relationship being so distant. I felt terrible that mom's passing didn't bring us together more. When I heard you'd been shot, I freaked. I wouldn't be able to forgive myself if you died without us ever resolving things. Not to be morbid, but that was my first thought."

"I'm so sorry about being an asshole when you were facing such a tough time. I just had ideas about what your future was supposed to be like, and I didn't know how to handle such an abrupt change. I'd like to keep working on our relationship if it's okay with you."

"Sure. I know how much you care about Ethan, so I've been thinking about making this happen for the last few years. I'm sorry too about being irresponsible and not making it easy on you. I think it's safe to say we both have regrets about everything. But I'd like to move on. I don't have a plan about how to do that, but I know that I want you involved in my life for more than just three-minute phone discussions and one paragraph emails."

She leaned on the bed and put an arm around him, just above his stomach. He felt a little pain but didn't say anything. They both cried silent tears, and the only sound in the room was his heart monitor. She pulled away and grabbed several tissues from the box on the bedside table. She handed a few to George.

"Okay, Dad, I'm gonna head out for now. I'll visit again tomorrow before I fly back to Massachusetts."

"Where are you staying? Would you like the keys to the house? You're welcome to stay there."

"No, that's not necessary. I'm at a hotel near the hospital. Thank you for the offer." She gave him a tight-lipped smile, her eyes still a pinkish-red hue. "Bye, dad."

"Bye, Liz. See ya later." He was overjoyed knowing that he could say that, and it was true.

CHAPTER TWENTY

THREE WEEKS LATER

The heatwave finally ended, but that didn't mean it was pleasant outside. It just meant that the climate in Mancheville had returned to the standard mugginess of a Pennsylvania summer. Fortunately, the air conditioning was functioning correctly again at Hank's. The timing of everything worked out pretty well. Nobody was interested in coming to Hank's right after the shooting; it just didn't feel right. After two days of almost no sales, the owners decided to shut the place down to allow an H.V.A.C. company to install a brand-new system. It was easier that way with no customers or employees in the way. The closure reignited people's desire to go to Hank's; something of an 'absence makes the heart grow fonder' type of thing.

Megan was manning her post when George finally made his return to Hank's. It was an unexciting night, but a healthy crowd for a Wednesday. All familiar faces. When George entered, it took a few moments for people to realize who it was. When they did, there was a rush of loud greetings, some clapping, and even whistles from Samuel and Patrick in the corner. Don was conspicuously missing, but that would be something that all of them would have to get used to for a while. It would be easier for some than others.

Erin rushed up to him and gave him a sweet, light squeeze. He looked over the top of her head and saw Mo with his hands cupped around his mouth, cheering for George like it was a sporting event. Megan dropped what she was doing and went over to a large bell customarily used to celebrate an exceptional tip. She pulled the rope handle, and it let out a loud ding that excited everyone even more. Alonso jumped from his stool and put an arm around George's shoulders, and declared, "I'll be the first one to buy George a drink. It's the least I can for my bodyguard! No arguments; first beer is on me." There were no disputes, and Megan popped the cap off a bottled beer and handed it to George.

"I'll put it on your tab, Alonso."

"Thanks, Megan!"

Patrick was soon by George's side. He bellowed, "If I can't get the first beer, I'd at least like to offer a toast in honor of our friend George!" George was never one to invite attention, so he was already mildly embarrassed by the hoopla. He blushed when Patrick mentioned a toast but held his hands out helplessly, not wanting to put a damper on the warm reception. Patrick went back to his place at the bar to grab his whiskey drink, then returned to the corner of the bar nearest the door where George was still standing—he hadn't made it more than five steps into the place yet.

Patrick cleared his throat and held his drink up high. "George, we're so relieved that you weren't hurt worse in the incident that took place here. And we're happy to see you back at Hank's. Everybody, raise your glass to our good friend, here." Everybody obeyed, even Megan. George hesitantly lifted his bottle. He couldn't get it past shoulder height without a pinch of pain, so he stopped there. When Patrick was satisfied that all glasses were up, he continued, "Here's health and prosperity, to you and all your posterity. And them that doesn't drink with sincerity, that they be damned for all eternity. Cheers!" A chorus of clinking glasses was followed by a moment of quiet while everybody took sizable gulps from their drinks. The room returned to its regular din, and George and Patrick went to where Samuel was sitting and took their place beside him.

George was seated between the two, so he faced forward and asked so both of them could hear, "How's Don?"

"I'm sure he'd love to know that you're asking. And that you're not pissed off at him." Samuel said the last part with a hint of a question in his voice as if he wasn't sure that George wasn't pissed off at Don.

"No, not pissed off. Maybe a little frustrated that he was stupid enough to get drunk with his gun on him at a bar. Disappointed in how he continues to let his knee-jerk reaction to things get him into trouble and, in this case, put his friends in danger. Mostly worried about what's going to happen to him. But pissed off? No, that's not how I would describe what I'm feeling."

Patrick looked at him with admiration. "It's not a surprise with you, George; you're one hell of a level-headed guy and a great friend not to be fuming at his bonehead move. I love the guy, but Jesus Christ, what an ordeal he caused. Can't say enough how thankful we are that the bullet didn't take you out, Georgy. You're a lucky son-of-a-bitch. So is Don, for that matter."

"Don has been holed up in his house other than going to the grocery store twice. I went to visit him, though. Even though he's avoiding people, he doesn't seem to be in too bad shape. He feels incredibly guilty, and he would not stop talking about how you probably hate him now. But he doesn't seem to be fretting too much about the punishment he's going to face. He has a court date in a month. I don't know the whole process, but I don't think that's his actual trial yet. I'm not sure he knows, but I think he has a decent lawyer." Samuel said it with some hope in his voice, but his face gave away his concern.

"Both Don's lawyer and the prosecuting attorney reached out to me, although that must have been before that court date was set. They both just asked me questions and had me recount whatever I could from the night. All I know is I told them both the same thing, and each said they'd eventually be back in touch with me as the case progressed."

Patrick just shook his head and remarked, "This is some wild shit."

George drank from his beer bottle until it was empty and set it gently on a coaster. "I think maybe I'll just leave Don alone for a while, just let him get everything figured out before visiting him or calling him. I think it's for the best. When you see him, just let him know that I forgive him, and I'm not mad. Will you do that, Sam?"

"Of course, George. I'm just glad that's the message I'm delivering."

"Thanks, Sam."

George vowed to himself at that point that he would tell everyone that he had been the one running the BrainSpot pages. He wasn't sure how much it even mattered at this point, but it felt like he should. It would be an interesting little nugget of gossip for Mancheville, so he could probably tell one person, and everybody would know in a day or so. Even so, he also promised himself that he would have a personal conversation with at least Don and Alonso about his bizarre involvement in their online conflict. They'd surely be confused as to his intentions and reasons for starting the pages. Somehow, George would have to explain that, but first, he'd have to figure it out himself.

He'd planned not to drink much, just to be safe with his wound still only about eighty percent healed. But he did have a few more bottles of lager while Patrick and Samuel caught him up on any town news that he'd missed during his stay at the hospital and subsequent time spent healing at home. He was not drunk but was buzzed enough that he felt an urge to address everybody still at Hank's. It was not a common urge for him, but he accepted it. He left enough cash on the bar for Megan to settle his tab and take a tip, then stood up and said, "Excuse me!" He had to say it one more time before all of the patrons turned their attention on him. Blood rushed to his head, and he started to feel a bit apprehensive, but he didn't sit back down.

"As you all know, it's been an exciting month for me. For all of us, really. A few weeks ago, what happened here was a terrible misunderstanding and mistake, and that's how I'm going to treat it. Getting angry just seems like a waste of time at this point. I'm going to heal and move on from what happened. Though it was a mistake, I can't ignore the animosity that built up over time between some folks in our town. It seemed just to get worse and worse this summer. I'm not saying it was directly the cause, but it certainly bred an environment where something awful was more likely to occur.

"I don't expect people always to get along. Arguments happen between people who care about each other. They get over it and refuse to let it ruin their relationship. Or, in some cases, disagreements occur because some people will just never like each other. That's reality. Either way, it's not pleasant when people don't see eye to eye. But if it's handled with at least a bit of civility—even if it's way back in the head and just barely present—chances are whatever is causing the rift will at some point become less important, and both parties can advance without a major emotional explosion.

"We can't ignore that getting online and using BrainSpot or other social media can feed negative feelings until you're continually creating twisted interpretations of your foe's every behavior. Context and nuance are non-existent, and everything that person does starts to seem like it's pointed directly at you. By its nature, the environment is conducive to developing a false reality and your own cultivated persona that is not necessarily based on truth. Add to that the fact that you're more likely to type something hurtful than you are to speak it when looking somebody in the eye, which creates a volatile situation.

"I'm not anti-technology. In fact, if you know me, you're probably aware that I love to use my computer and even worked in technology before I retired. I'm an old guy, but not one that automatically dismisses anything new as lousy. As far as social media and online communication, I'm admittedly not as comfortable with it as a younger person might be who grew up with it. That's to be expected. But I do genuinely believe that there are rewards to it when used right. It's just that we all need to figure out what that means. I think we will. I don't know what it looks like since I'm not a fortune teller or a tech genius. But there's no doubt that it needs some refining.

"I'm aware that I have a reputation as a pretty nice, honest, and virtuous guy. I'm proud of that, and I'm glad people see me that way, but I have my weak moments. Like anybody, I've done things in life that I'm not proud of, and they've caused me pain. I had a stable job that got me to a relatively comfortable retirement, a great marriage to my wife Anna, and friends that always kept me sane and still support me to this day. But something was missing in my life for a while, mainly because of my lack of humility and inability to forgive. As strange as it sounds, that something is back in my life because of this weird incident. It's wonderful, but it also reminds me that if I'd been a little better of a person, I would not have been missing it for so long. And that's what it's all about. I didn't mess up because of social media. It didn't even really exist when I screwed up, at least not as we know it now. The problem was my lazy communication and how I built up ideas of who I was without considering how that affected other people I loved. I'm lucky that I got another chance. Not everybody is so fortunate.

"I'm going to end with that. I'm not as comfortable as Pat talking in front of everybody. I'm now feeling a tad embarrassed with my blabbering. But I still mean what I said. I'm going to head home for the night. My daughter and grandson are visiting tomorrow, and I'd like to make sure I'm plenty rested to spend the day with them. Thanks for making me feel appreciated tonight. Cheers and good night." He drank the last of his beer and started for the door, swapping several handshakes and goodbyes before finally making it outside to begin his walk home.

CHAPTER TWENTY-ONE

George, Elizabeth, and Ethan walked on the asphalt path that horseshoed around the cemetery. It held a multitude of cracks that looked like tree roots. Larger grooves split off into systems of small erratic lines. Sporadically, there were spots where multiple cracks had met, and there was an entire chunk missing. Certain areas had subtle dips and bowls where the asphalt wasn't supported properly. When it rained, they collected water and became puddles. It needed repair, but it still served its purpose well enough, so the Mancheville powers-that-be hadn't yet made plans to resurface the path.

Due to the path's condition, Elizabeth was concerned that her father would trip or stumble and possibly reopen the wound on his side. She hooked her arm in his, and they walked beside each other at a languid pace. Ethan walked much faster ahead of them, darting in and out of rows of gravestones to read names that sounded interesting or familiar to him. He'd detour off the path, then return to it without ever getting behind his slow-moving mom and grandpa. George didn't need Elizabeth's help, and his wound was nearly healed, but he didn't decline her arm. He wasn't going to turn down the opportunity for close contact and a pleasant walk with his daughter.

Moments later, they came to the row where Anna's stone was located. George was somewhat surprised when Elizabeth turned first and led him into the row. The funeral service was nearly two years ago, and he wasn't sure if she'd been back to Anna's grave since then. Ethan had passed Anna's row and made his way back to them by cutting through three other rows. He walked carefully to avoid accidentally stepping on any of the flowers or decorations that people had placed near headstones. The three of them arrived simultaneously at Anna's grave and stopped in front of it. They were silent for a good two minutes, all of them reading and rereading the words and numbers cut into the granite. Below her name, there were three lines of text. One line held the dates of her life. The next one had a quote that she'd requested be put on her stone. The final one was an attribution to the author of the passage.

April 3, 1948-September 25, 2016
"Life without love is like a tree without blossoms or fruit."
– Khalil Gibran

Ethan broke the silence and said in a soft, deferential tone, "I remember when she used to take me out into the garden with her. I loved it, but I never listened to what she tried to tell me about growing stuff. I liked seeing all of the different colors of vegetables, all their different shapes, and stuff. And she let me throw the vegetables that were damaged, rotten, or chewed on by rabbits against the huge oak tree in the backyard. They'd explode into a bunch of gooey chunks that scattered in the yard around the tree. Then we'd rake the pieces, pick them up by hand, and put them in a bucket that we'd empty into the compost pile. It's a good memory, but now I wish I'd have paid more attention to what she was teaching me about growing stuff. I might grow a garden someday, but I'll probably have to learn from somebody on the internet that didn't know as much as grandma."

"She certainly had a green thumb," George said quietly.

"Huh, what is that?"

Both Elizabeth and George laughed. George explained, "I guess that's kind of an older phrase. It just means she was good at growing plants—an expert in gardening. It's more than just being knowledgeable; it's as if it also comes naturally to the person. Exactly like it was with your grandma."

"I see. Yeah, that was definitely her."

Elizabeth added, "When I was little, she used to win all the time for things she entered into the county fair. All kinds of stuff; tomatoes, pumpkins, carrots. I can't even remember all of it."

"Wow, I haven't thought about that in years. She got tired of it and stopped, probably when you were in high school."

"Yep, tenth grade, I think."

"She kept growing stuff. She didn't care to enter it anymore. Honestly, I think she got upset the last year she entered because she thought something was unfair. She was sure she was gonna win the pickle contest. You had to grow your own cucumbers and make your own brine and all that stuff. Those cucumbers were her special garden project, and she read everything she could about growing them perfectly. She was proud as hell of the pickles that she ended up making. I think they were garlic dill or something. When she got second, she insisted that the fix was in because the winner was friends with the judge. Anna never entered another damn thing in the fair contests. Isn't it funny the things we let bother us sometimes? She was not a confrontational person, but she was ready to fight the winner that day. Or the judge. Maybe both!" The three of them laughed together, no longer feeling the need to be solemn. "She may have been right. The two ladies involved were very, very good friends. It was pretty suspect. It was Betty Anders and Sarah Ross. Do you remember them, Liz?"

"Mm, vaguely, but not really."

"They're in their eighties now. I think they had a falling out at some point and don't even talk to each other anymore. But they're both still around. Maybe Betty finally got tired of being pressured to vote for Sarah's vegetables at the fair."

The trio laughed again before settling into another silence, this time with more pleasant, smiling faces. The sun was beginning to set over the tops of the trees where the trail was located. The sky was glowing with purplish-pink cotton candy hues and the occasional warm gash of yellowy-orange. George looked at the horizon even though it was still bright enough to sting his eyes a bit. It was beautiful, and for it, and because of his current company, and for what he was lucky to experience with Anna, he was grateful. He looked into the remnants of the sun until his eyes could no longer take it. He moved them back down to the front of Anna's stone. Bending down, George removed the now decrepit lily that he'd brought last time he'd visited Anna. He had nothing to replace it with but made a mental note to find a new flower at home and soon get it to her grave.

"Looking back, I can't believe how much mom and I used to go at it. When I was a teenager, especially from the ages of about thirteen to sixteen, it was just a constant struggle between her and me."

"I certainly remember that. I just tried to stay out of the way with most things."

"We argued about boys, clothes, partying, schoolwork, and just about anything else you can imagine. It's so embarrassing to remember how I acted sometimes. Not to say I was wrong about everything, but even when I was right, I acted like such a brat."

"That was sometimes true, but I don't think you were much worse than the average teenager. It's a difficult time for everybody."

"By my senior year of high school, she and I had become much closer, and we both backed off each other a little bit. I finally got comfortable telling her personal stuff, and she was way more understanding than I ever thought she would be. And she shared things about her own life that often surprised me. Nothing bad or shocking, just little things that I never expected from her."

George watched Elizabeth as she spoke, noticing how much neater her appearance was compared to the last time he'd seen her in the hospital. She must have reacted quickly to the news of the shooting accident and went to Pennsylvania with no concern for outward appearance, which George found both flattering and heartwarming. Now, even in simple army green shorts and a beige tank top, she had a chic, stylish air of a confident middle-aged woman. It was much more visible now to George than it was in the hospital. Her hair was a complicated array of thick curly layers that she frequently lifted to let air reach her neck. Elizabeth embraced her natural curls. Anna had the same kind of hair before it turned more dry and weak at some point in her sixties. Even when it was thick and curly, she'd always straightened it, saying that she didn't want to deal with such a mess of coils and waves that never seemed to cooperate with her attempts at styling it. He couldn't recall specifically, but he'd bet that there was at least one knock-down-drag-out fight about hairstyles between Anna and Elizabeth.

He looked at the purse that Elizabeth had that was slung low and rested on her hip. It had some age to it, and George recognized it from decades earlier. She'd owned it since her adolescence. It was a simple canvas-like material, purple in color and minimal in design. He wasn't sure what kind of style it was; it looked like a small tote bag but had a flap that covered the top. The flap could be secured with a single red button. There were two matching buttons sewn on the flap for decoration. There was a tiny cluster of string in the area between the two buttons where another one had been. George was immediately reminded of the button lying on top of Anna's gravestone weeks earlier, a perfect match for the buttons on Elizabeth's purse. He checked to see if it was still there, but it wasn't.

He considered that it might be some secret that Elizabeth had with Anna, perhaps a memory or something meaningful from the past, that had made her intentionally rip off the button and put it on the stone herself. Some kind of token of her love. Maybe there was a story about the purse and the button that George should remember but had lost to aging. Of course, the button really could have just mistakenly popped off and fallen from her purse, and somebody passing by had seen it in the grass and sat it on the nearest gravestone. George could logically conclude that Elizabeth had indeed visited Anna's grave since the funeral, but he didn't know how or why the button had ended up on her stone. He didn't ask Elizabeth; he might do it someday.

CHAPTER TWENTY-TWO

FOUR YEARS LATER

Even while pleasantly tinking their bottles together, it occurred to George that it could be the last time he'd see Ethan for a very long time. It was unlikely—but not impossible—that he might never see him again. Putting the entire country between them essentially meant placing a logistical challenge on seeing each other that could easily strain their relationship. Nobody knows what will happen to their familial and social connections when they move far away. Realistically, 'out of sight, out of mind' is the idiom that applies to long-distance relationships more often than 'absence makes the heart grow fonder."

George didn't want to be negative; his goal in bringing Ethan to Hank's was to give him a nice sendoff for his move to Seattle. He'd graduated college with honors and spent a year and a half interning and cutting his teeth at entry-level jobs around the Boston area while living with his parents. Now he was moving to Seattle to work for a major tech firm, a transition that was both daunting and exciting for him.

Ethan was more than optimistic about maintaining strong relationships with his grandpa, parents, and friends. George had seen too many people move away with the same sincere intentions, who then disappeared for decades or indefinitely, not to be somewhat jaded about the whole thing. He despised those thoughts, trying his best to remind himself that his bond with Ethan was one of the strongest he knew of between a grandfather and grandchild.

It should be different with Ethan, and it was, but it didn't feel quite different enough to let George be pleased about the move. Stored deep away inside his emotions, George even felt a bit angry that Ethan was moving so far away. And it wasn't just a physical move. Barring any setbacks, a job like the one Ethan had procured put him on a track to make more money and be better off than George had ever dreamed of for himself. George's comfortable life in a small town like Mancheville was simply not on the same plane as success in the tech industry in a major metropolitan area. It wasn't fair to Ethan to have those feelings, and George would absolutely never bring them up, but they were still there. He'd not felt them before, only now experiencing them with Ethan's big changes. He desperately hoped that he could hide them enough to enjoy his last night with Ethan before the young man made his relocation to Seattle.

After several sips in silence, Ethan asked, "So how have things been with you and mom?"

"Really good. Especially lately. I've had some of the happiest years of my life recently. It's been wonderful after losing your grandma. Your mom has visited me pretty regularly."

"That's great. Kind of sad, I guess, that I don't talk with her much these days. I've stayed pretty busy with work, and when I'm not doing that, I'm usually out with friends. Haven't visited you as much as I should have in recent years either. Sorry about that."

"Don't worry about it. You've got a lot going on trying to establish yourself in adult life. I understand."

"So, you and mom have been good?"

"We have. It was great when we reconnected after the accident. We talked several times a week on the phone, and we visited each other a bunch of times in the first six months or so. Honestly, it got a little rough when we eventually opened up about old stuff. It's not easy to revisit those old feelings. If you think they go away, you'd be wrong."

George didn't say it to Ethan, but he wasn't sure a relationship between a parent and child could ever really be the same after a significant gap of time apart. It's only natural for a child to feel abandoned by a parent in such a situation. No matter how hard a child pushes away, it's hard not to feel like it's always the parent's job to make the situation right, no matter what it takes. At the same time, a parent may feel like their child is ungrateful for all of the sacrifices they made to bring them into the world and provide them what they needed to survive. Maybe a parent feels like the universe, or God, or Mother Earth, or whatever metaphysical thing exists, let them down by not providing perpetual patience and understanding to make them the perfect parent.

"My dad has been encouraging about me moving to Seattle. She's been pretty silent about it. She isn't silent about telling me that I go out to the bar too much with my friends. And she wasn't a fan of the girl I was dating for a year or so. She wasn't quiet about that either. She didn't make it easy for that to continue, which was part of the reason it didn't. To be fair, it probably wasn't going anywhere anyway."

George licked some beer foam off his upper lip and said evenly, "I'm not going to pretend that anything I say will make it easy to deal with her at this point in your life. Two people's issues with each other are their own, and you'll have to figure that out with her. I can only give you some simple advice, and you can do with it what you will. Get pissed at her, tell her when she's overstepping boundaries, and do what you think is best for you, even if she disagrees. Just don't sever the connection. I promise it's not worth it. You might even be tempted to do it because, in the back of your mind, you can always go back to normal if you want to. It's a very real possibility that you can't, and you won't. Not for a long time and maybe not ever. Oh, and just admit you're wrong every now and then. Out loud and clearly. You don't have to do it every time you're wrong. That's hard as hell. Just fess up to a mistake or say you're sorry every once in a while. That goes for every relationship you have, by the way."

Ethan wordlessly drank but nodded his head to acknowledge that he'd heard George. After a few beats of silence, he asked, "Where are all of the people you usually drink with? I don't recognize anybody here. I feel bad that I've barely visited in the last four years. When I have, it's been so short that I don't get to see any of your friends."

"It's an unusual night, now that you mention it. I still talk to the same people you always knew, for the most part. They just happen not to be around tonight. Let's see. You probably remember Sam. He's the same old guy. He likes to go hunting. We still go golfing together. He doesn't come to the bar as much anymore. I think his wife got tired of him being out at the bar every night. She makes him play board games every Thursday and take her out for a dinner date at a decent restaurant outside of Mancheville at least once a week."

The thought of Samuel being forced to play Monopoly and become a foodie made them both laugh.

"There's Patrick, of course. He was about as committed a friend as possible after the shooting. He was genuinely concerned about my well-being and made sure to visit me at the hospital and at home every day while recuperating. That being said, I think he was pleased that he had a new tale to add to his barroom repertoire. For a while, he recounted the night of the shooting to anybody that hadn't been there. He and his wife Charlene are still together and celebrated their fiftieth wedding anniversary last year. They took a cruise to the Caribbean and renewed their vows. They're still out almost every night at the places around town. Probably will be until they can't physically do it."

"What about that young couple that was at the concert we went to years ago. I don't remember their names offhand."

"Oh, sure, Mo and Erin! They're still together and live in town. Mo has done well for himself at the same place he was working at when you met him. They make bottles and plastic packaging and stuff, I think. Anyway, he was promoted to a manager position and seems to like it there. Erin is back at her H.R. job at the steel plant after taking some time off to have their first baby. Ellen Grace Darwish is her full name, if I remember correctly. Once Erin was about a third of the way through her pregnancy, they announced it to everybody here. Of course, Patrick gave an elaborate toast, and everybody bought them drinks—just orange juice for Erin. I imagine the baby will be turning one soon. Obviously, with the baby, they haven't been around quite as much as they used to be. I still see them occasionally, though. They're good people."

Megan stopped in front of their empty glasses and gestured towards them with her chin. George nodded without a word. She flipped her bar rag over her shoulder to free both hands and grabbed their glasses.

"As you can probably tell, Megan still holds the crown as the best bartender in town."

"Aw shucks, George," said Megan playfully after overhearing his compliment. "That's very nice, but it won't get you any free beer!"

Ethan laughed while George put on a fake disappointed frown. When Megan returned with their now full glasses, she set them down gently and muttered, "Okay, fine, these two are on me, but only because I was eavesdropping earlier and heard you talking about Ethan migrating to the west coast." She slapped her hand down on the bar beside Ethan's hand for emphasis and said in a louder voice, "Safe travels and all the best to you!"

They both warmly thanked her and took giant slugs of beer. Megan gave them a wink and went back to work.

"She is awesome. I've been lucky enough to get to know her better after some late-night talks. I'm glad they're treating her right here. They gave her a healthy raise after the night I was shot. It really could have gotten out of control. She not only kept the patrons relatively calm; she also assisted the first responders and handled it as well as anybody could have. Believe it or not, she got a husband from that night too. One of the E.M.T.s on the scene had noticed Megan. He was both impressed by her calmness under pressure and smitten by her good looks."

"That's crazy! What a weird night," said Ethan, shaking his head.

"It really was. Megan said that the E.M.T. remained professional and did his job on the scene but must have tucked away a mental note to return to Hank's to meet her properly. Even in the madness, she'd also noticed him. He had a firm but reassuring way about him that alleviated a lot of the situation's pressure. Megan also added that he had some pretty nice tattooed biceps and a well-groomed beard, which didn't hurt his chances of catching her attention. They struck up a romantic relationship and were married in a small outdoor ceremony less than a year later. Strange how things happen."

"And what about Don and Alonso? Did Don get locked up? Did Alonso try to get revenge, or anything, after Don shot at him? They both seemed a little whacked out."

"During his last semester at college, Alonso cut his drinking down to only the weekends. He was already doing okay in his classes, but he excelled with a clearer head and more time to study. He completed all of the classes he needed to get his associate degree in nursing and immediately started working a retirement home. Within a year, he decided to pursue a bachelor's degree through an accelerated program while continuing to work at the home. He finished the coursework in the expected one and a half year time span while still doing great at his job."

George took a swallow of beer and continued, "Armed with his degree and several glowing performance reviews, he explored the nursing job market and found something that piqued his interest. The position was for a traveling nurse who would visit several patients a day to provide homecare. He was offered the job and accepted it. It turned out to be the perfect role for him. He avoids getting annoyed with coworkers and impulsively insulting them by not having any coworkers. He likes to concentrate on his patients and treat them without running into disagreements with other nurses about how to do it. He answers to just one boss who is happy not to micromanage him. He loves driving around to different places, is paid well for it, and has a relatively flexible schedule.

"Alonso's family was fortunate to avoid the catastrophe of him being shot. They weren't as lucky with his brother. When Alonso visited me in the hospital, he was also there for his brother, a drug addict. On the same night of the shooting, his brother had a fatal overdose of heroin laced with fentanyl. His girlfriend also overdosed, but she survived and later went to rehab. Alonso's family never spoke to her again. Unfortunately, Alonso didn't make it to the hospital in time to see this brother alive one more time.

"But everybody reacts to tragedy differently. Alonso, happily, turned his grief into motivation to better himself as a way to honor his brother. He admitted that he also felt great relief at not having to worry about his brother every day. The spinning thoughts in his head ceased, the knot of concern in his stomach disappeared, and a big weight was lifted from his shoulders. He was still Alonso, but without the excess agitation affecting his behavior."

Ethan looked surprised but also genuinely happy for Alonso. "Man, that is rough. Shot at for no reason and a brother dying in one night. I can't believe he didn't go crazy."

"I can't either. He was always so tightly wound I would have assumed the slightest thing could have made him go to a dark place. For some reason, he seemed to need a tragedy to clarify things about his life. That's the only I can describe it."

"And Don, whatever happened with him?" Ethan was now rapt, listening to his grandpa's updates about his friends and acquaintances from Mancheville.

It delighted George, and he happily moved on to Don. "He faced a charge of 'assault with a deadly weapon' after injuring me. He was facing as much as ten years in prison if he received a maximum sentence. He did have a few things working in his favor. First, he didn't flee and was cooperative with the police when they arrived at Hank's. Second, I was not seriously wounded, which could have doubled the maximum sentence. Lastly, the judge considered that everybody in the bar, even people who admitted they didn't care for him, acknowledged that they believed Don sincerely thought Alonso was pointing a gun at Megan. There was a consensus that he'd fired in what he thought was a defense of Megan, himself, and others at Hank's. As part of a plea deal, he received only two and a half years in prison and a year of probation. As it was a felony, he also lost the right to own any guns.

"What happened with those two after the shooting ended up being the weirdest part of it all. And this is all true; 100%. I've talked to both of them in great detail, and I've seen it with my own eyes. They developed an unlikely but sincere friendship. They maintained contact for the duration of Don's time in prison with letters, private messaging on BrainSpot, and even an occasional in-person visit. Their conflicting views on many issues didn't change much. Half of their correspondence ended up being arguments about politics, religion, or whatever divisive topic was popular at any given time. And music. They discovered that their musical tastes were something else they could bicker about if they ran out of other topics.

"There was one major difference, though. They held each other to one stringent rule that neither could venture off-topic into personal insults or remarks made only to upset the other person. Both stuck by it and only had to be checked by the other person on the rarest of occasions. Their exchanges blossomed into the most unlikely of friendships, and both were better for it.

"Believe it or not, it gets even stranger. They became so close to each other that they developed a plan to run a business together when they released Don from jail. Their plan sprung from the idea that Mancheville needed a proper coffee shop, which they both happened to agree upon. Don didn't drink in prison, which was easy when the main alcohol option was wine made in toilets. Alonso significantly lowered his consumption to better focus on school and eventually his career. They both found that replacing beer, wine, and liquor with coffee was an easy way to abstain or limit their alcohol intake. That led to an enthusiastic discussion about the need for a spot in Mancheville to get decent coffee because the gas stations weren't cutting it.

"The business plan was realistic because Alonso had access to some seed money from an unexpected source. Years before his death, Alonso's brother had been offered life insurance at one of the rare restaurants that he cooked at that offered benefits to employees. He worked there during a clean period in his life and stayed long enough to get benefits. Despite his substance abuse background, he could sign up for a policy, and a small amount of money was deducted from his paycheck every two weeks. He never thought about it again after signing up for it on a whim. After his death, the lawyer who handled his affairs discovered the policy and believed that the beneficiary was legally entitled to the insurance payout. After he proved that Alonso's brother had been completely honest about his health and drug behavior on his application, and was still offered the policy, the insurance company was forced to pay out the full sum. That $150,000 would eventually help fund the opening of the Quarreler's Corner Coffee Shop, with Alonso and Don as the proprietors. Alonso is mostly a silent partner but helps out occasionally because he has the freedom to move his nursing schedule around. Don does most of the work of buying supplies and equipment, hiring workers, and arranging the advertising. He also does any necessary repairs to their building or arranges contractors to do the larger jobs that he can't handle on his own. They opened to rousing success, and they sustain their business by hosting various gatherings for AA, veteran fellowship, cancer survivors, community event planning, paint nights, and just about anything else people wanted to do together while they drank coffee and tea and ate pastries."

Ethan's mouth hung open like a cartoon character. He shook his head in amazement and said, "Never in a million years would I have guessed that was what ended up happening with those two!" He threw his head back and let out a huge belly laugh.

George couldn't contain his wide grin, especially when he added, "And I'm the admin for the Quarreler's Corner BrainSpot page. I got rid of the U.S.A. Conservative Life and Progressive Effort pages and instead use that time to do casual marketing things like spreading the word about upcoming events and coordinating the schedule for the groups that meet at the coffee shop."

Ethan laughed again and said simply, "Unreal."

George, still grinning, just shrugged and remarked, "Life is odd sometimes. A lot of the time, actually."

"Grandpa, I loved the updates on your crew here in town, but I think I should stop drinking before it gets too late. I have to leave early to start my drive out to Seattle."

Yep, I think it's time for me to tap out for the night anyway. I'll just settle up with Megan, and then we can head home."

Ethan poked around in his wallet, but it was evident that there wasn't much to be found. "I have five bucks if that helps," he offered.

"Put your damn money away. You know it's no good here when you're with me," said George with a fake stern tone. He grinned, happy to have at least one more moment where Ethan still felt a little bit childlike and powerless. George paid in cash and waved off the change from Megan.

"We'll see about that next time I visit after I have some paychecks in the bank. I'm buying even if I have to sneak money to Megan when you're not looking."

George followed Ethan out the door, close enough that he could reach out with both of his arms and grab his shoulders and shake him playfully. He ignored the brief jag of pain in his side from lifting his arms high enough to reach Ethan's shoulders that were up taller than his. They walked for a block in the muted incandescence of the streetlights that spread wide but didn't illuminate anything fully. George still lagged behind Ethan, careful not to trip over the uneven sidewalk squares that he knew from experience were outside Hank's. The next block had a sidewalk only a year or so old, and George was able to use the safer surface to pull even with Ethan. George walked at a pace faster than what came naturally anymore while Ethan slowed down as indiscernibly as possible so that they could walk side-by-side the rest of the way back to George's home.

CHAPTER TWENTY-THREE

As it always does, time quelled interest in the shooting incident at Hank's. Mancheville lived on with nary a thought of the event only a few years later. A couple more coats of paint have been put on the brick buildings around town. The asphalt path in the cemetery was repaired when pieces as large as Frisbees started separating from the rest of the asphalt. The department store finally closed, but the grocery store and hardware store remain in operation. Things change, but not quickly or dramatically, which is why most of the people in Mancheville live there.

At some point, a well-known travel blogger happened to visit The Mancheville Pub. She featured the pub in a top 25 list of her favorite small bars and restaurants in Pennsylvania. It attracted new customers, both local and non-locals traveling through the area. It was a very unexpected but welcome boost for them. Nick continued to work long nights in his small office, solving the myriad of puzzles that came with keeping the business in the black. Some press to bolster the pub was excellent, and it let Nick breathe a little bit easier, but it wasn't what would ultimately sustain them.

The Night's Quest, building on the success of their steak night, added a seafood night. The freshest seafood they could get their hand on, like shrimp, flounder, crabs, seabass, mussels, and just about anything else imaginable. The selection varied each week but was always of excellent quality. Customers responded, and it became another indefinite weekly special for the Night's Quest. They gained a seafood night, but they lost their best server and bartender when they moved to New Orleans together. The older crowd grumbled and complained vigorously about their replacements. Service was slow, their steaks came out the wrong way, and the seafood tasted like it had been sitting too long. Patrick frequently commented on the new bartender's light hand with the gin, requesting another splash nearly every time he tasted a fresh drink. And yet, by six months into their employment, the dining crowd was on a first-name basis with the newest waiter, and Patrick was toasting Morris Lee with the new bartender—full story included, of course.

Late at night, Hank's is still the meeting spot for the most committed drinkers in Mancheville. The shooting barely put a dent in the business. It probably increased the cachet of the place in the long run. The hole from the bullet that grazed George was repaired very soon after the shooting, and it's impossible to tell where it once was. When it comes up in conversation, a Hank's customer will sometimes claim that they know precisely where the bullet had pierced the wall. Usually, with a few drinks inside their belly, the person spins around and bounds off their stool, anxious to point out the exact place where it entered. They're almost always wrong. Most who say they know where it is weren't even present on the night of the shooting, and they're working from a secondhand account of it. Traces of the repaired bullet hole can't be found by physical or visual inspection because there are so many marks on the wall where tables and chairs rubbed against it, guitar cases and amps bumped into it, the occasional splash of beer spilled on it, and various other forms of mild—but consistent—abuse had occurred. The truth is, nobody knows for sure where the bullet went into the wall anymore, even if they swear up and down that they do. Everybody has their opinion about it, and it's been known to cause an argument or two.

ACKNOWLEDGEMENTS

I owe much appreciation to my early-draft readers, Amy Fuddy and Jeff Leggett, for their honest feedback and confidence-restoring encouragement.

Lots of love to my family: Mom, Dad, Justin, Jennifer, Laura, Mike, uncles, aunts, cousins, nephews, and nieces.

To Mika: I love you even if this is the only page you read.

Thanks to Chris Fenwick for editing this book and establishing my relationship with Sunbury Press.

To Sue Petersen: Thanks for igniting the writing spark in me.

ABOUT THE AUTHOR

Job Tyler Leach grew up in Bainbridge, PA, and now resides in East Petersburg, PA. He graduated from Millersville University with a Bachelor of Arts in English and a minor in Sociology. In addition to writing fiction, Job writes professionally in the marketing and E-Commerce field. As the Raven Flies is his first novel, and Wilting at Gin Mills is his second, both published under the Milford House imprint of Sunbury Press.

www.jobtylerleach.com

https://www.facebook.com/JobLeachWriter
https://twitter.com/leach_job